I0630096

AFTER THE FALL

APOCALYPSE CHRONICLES
BOOK 6

DARREL SPARKMAN

ROUGH
EDGES
PRESS

Rough Edges Press
An Imprint of Wolfpack Publishing
9850 S. Maryland Parkway, Suite A-5 #323
Las Vegas, Nevada 89183

roughedgespress.com

Paperback ISBN 978-1-68549-317-2
eBook ISBN 978-1-68549-316-5
LCCN 2023940008

AFTER THE FALL

Like flowery fields the nations stand,
Pleased with the morning light-
The flowers beneath the mower's hand,
Lay withering in the night.

—Isaac Watts, 1719

THE FALL

THE MAN DRESSED in black stood on a balcony overlooking the inside floor of a vast warehouse in the waterfront district of New York City. Seeing his reflection in the glass partition separating the balcony from the rest of the warehouse, he noticed how stark his long blond hair looked against his black shirt—and the black background behind him. Black. It was fitting.

"How much longer?" he asked of the man named Krueger standing beside him. Krueger was a mercenary and good at his job. The man in black had used him before.

"Soon." Krueger shook his head. "The last group will be here in a few minutes. They are stuck in traffic."

"Who is coming?" He noted Kruger's manner was casual and his eyes cold and lifeless.

"We have representatives from sleeper cells in nearly every state. They will carry out the most important missions. The rest are a mixed bag. Patriots. Survivalists. Posse and Aryans. All trained and willing." Krueger chuckled, but somehow it didn't sound funny. "We even have several religious groups looking to help their god with the end times."

"How many in all?"

"We have over a hundred people—all sworn to secrecy about their assignments. They won't even talk to each other."

"Do they know the real purpose of our cause?"

"Some might guess, but most won't. They know only what we tell them, and even that is tempered by what they wish to believe."

The man in black turned and pierced the other man with his cold gaze. "You told me all was in readiness. I've brought the weapons. Disappointment at this juncture in time will *not* be tolerated."

"Take it easy. Relax. Our cause is theirs. They all want simpler lives. All of them distrust the government. To a man, they believe the collapse of the United States is inevitable. So, why not make it come sooner, at a time when they are prepared for it and can control it?"

"Do they actually think they can retain control? Really?" The mocking voice of the man in black echoed softly in the empty room.

"I don't believe they understand the scope of what we are doing or how quickly the end will come." Krueger gestured toward a few of the men below who, even in this gathering, were openly carrying weapons. "And some couldn't care less." He looked at the man dressed in black. "Your predictions? The two weeks? It seems such a short time."

Ice-blue eyes surveyed him, then glanced away. Hands linked behind his back, legs spread slightly, the man in black prepared to lecture him, knowing in advance he was one of those who didn't care.

"Not really," the man in black replied. "It is actually very simple." He held up his fingers, one at a time. "Food. Transport. Fuel. Electrical power. If we interrupt these things for just a few weeks, the collapse will come. Nothing can stop it."

"But in two weeks?" His normally calm demeanor collapsed for a moment.

"Ultimately, it's the food." The man in black looked exasperatedly at the other man. "Most stores carry at most a two-week supply of canned goods. Some have more, some less. Perishable goods will spoil more quickly. So, if there's no electricity to run the refrigerators, everything will spoil. People won't be able to eat the meat quickly enough, and most people won't even understand that they should try."

Krueger's interest was fully piqued. "Portable generators?"

"Where do you get the fuel to run them? And there are not enough of them, even when there is a small power outage. Gas pumps need power. Hand pumps take a long time, and by then, people will be killing for possession of what above-ground tanks there are. If the trucks of the transport industry have no fuel and cannot deliver, then the masses will be hungry. Even though people can go several weeks without eating, they will be hungry in three days. Hungry people do terrible, desperate things."

The man in black smiled mirthlessly at Krueger. "There will be millions of hungry people."

"What of the government agencies?"

"Ah, you must be a liberal progressive, always wanting the government to bail you out. Oh, the government will try to cope. FEMA and the Red Cross will send people to assess the situation. By the time they get everything mobilized and realize they must release their own stockpiles of fuel and start food drops, it will be too late. The same problems will apply to other countries. They will try to help, but it will be too late. There simply won't be time."

"In the end, what is it you hope to achieve?"

The man in black turned a cold smile on him. "Chaos. Nothing less."

Krueger pointed toward the floor of the warehouse. "The last group has arrived."

The man in black stepped impatiently toward the door. "Then let it begin."

———

LATER, after the warehouse was empty, the man in black thought of what they had put into motion.

Two weeks.

Handheld tactical weapons couldn't penetrate the nuclear and hydroelectric power stations. Everyone knew that. All the elite think tanks and experts had proclaimed the premise impossible and scoffed at the possibility, so everyone believed it. Facilities were hardened and guarded. The security around all key facilities was always on high alert.

The solution was simple. Terrorists would detonate small tactical nukes around the perimeter of their targets to take out all the trunk lines delivering electricity from the power stations. The surrounding area would remain so hot with radiation repairs would be impossible. The nation would go dark.

The government kept huge stockpiles of fuel, but would refuse to allocate it to the transportation system, which delivers and disperses most of the food to the country. With the world in a state of chaos, and fearing an imminent attack from abroad, the United States Government would confiscate all shipments of fuel and earmark it for the military. And without electricity, only fuel stored in above-ground tanks could be easily and quickly obtained by the people. In less than a week, the largest transportation system in the world would stop moving.

Millions of people living in the huge metropolitan areas have to buy food every day from markets or restaurants to survive.

Millions of people will get hungry.

Millions of people will begin to move.

There was no place to go.

People will die.

Millions...

Within the first year, at least 80 percent of the population will be gone. The mass graves dug by the military would make the killing fields of Cambodia look like scout camp. After a time, even the military units stop trying to cope, and pull back to the east and west coasts, reasoning that the coastal waters could support at least a rudimentary existence. Of course, the coastal fish are full of iodine and mercury, but death in the distant future is an abstract thought when you are hungry.

The interior of the United States, from the Alleghenies to the Rockies, will be on its own. Experts predict that the rule will be survival of the fittest, but in fact it's mostly survival of the lucky.

The man in black looked around the bleak and empty warehouse. He knew he wouldn't survive. It didn't matter.

ONE

TWENTY YEARS LATER...

A COVEY of quail exploded into the air, leaving the clump of bushes they hid under with rocket-like force. Startled sumac leaves rustled frantically, as small brown feathers drifted slowly to the ground in the filtered sunlight washing over the small clearing in the forest.

John Trent kicked free of the stirrups and left the saddle of his horse in a long dive, rolling up behind a log next to the trail. After the initial flurry of movement, he became completely still. He tried to blink away the sweat trickling into his eyes. A black wood ant, flushed from the crumbling bark of the log, crawled across his knuckles. He still didn't move. This was the new frontier. The first to move often became the first to die, and he didn't intend to die.

He cast a quick glance at his horse standing a few feet away—a horse that seemed very unconcerned with the actions of its master. A big help you are. The horse didn't glance his way, entertained instead by cropping grass at the edge of the trail and swatting flies with its tail. Bunched clumps of tall fescue seemed to be the only thing holding the horse's attention. The roan gelding seemed unaware of any danger, and it was usually a good watchdog. Maybe something else had flushed the birds. Maybe a fox, or coyote. Maybe.

He sighed as his worried glance went to the leather saddlebags draped over the horse, stamped US Army. If someone wanted the courier bags, they would try for the horse right away. He'd been a courier between the few remaining Army outposts left on the new frontier for the last three years. Documents in the bag were of little interest to most folks. What was left of the remaining standing Army of the old United States was impotent at best, rarely conjuring up anything but disdain and contempt.

That left one other alternative. Someone wanted him, and not for a moment did he consider any other option. There were hunters out there, and he was the prey.

Trent took stock of his weapons. The black AK47 with its thirty-round magazine slung over the saddle horn and as far away as next week's rabbit stew. He carried Kalashnikov's finest because it always worked. Always. The .45 caliber single-action Ruger Vaquero was in his belly holster for the same reason. Revolvers rarely jam. His fighting knife and a sore shoulder from rolling over the log were all he had with him. They'd have to do.

In the old books, the hero would whistle for his horse, and it would come bounding up, eager to help save the day. *This horse would end up miles away if he whistled at it.*

Normal sounds gradually came back to the forest, creeping on silent feet and whispering in the wind. The curious brown thrush and raucous blue jays finally went about their business, throwing disgusted looks back at the bushes where nothing was moving anymore. It was hard for them to be nature's sentinels when there was nothing to see.

In the distance, Trent could hear a mockingbird making its idiot calls. Closer in, a marmot came out of its burrow, nose up to the wind, red fur shimmering in the sun, deciding it was safe to go back to digging roots. A bumblebee came and went in an avalanche of sound shattering the silence. Its fat body tagged by scientists as being unable to fly, the bee navigated effortlessly through the trees.

Cursing silently, chiding himself for not keeping better watch, he began a slow scan around the surrounding forest. The day was hot, too hot for early May, and the small brown lizard perched on the log just inches from his eyes panted to rid itself of the heat. Looking at the lizard directed his eyes to the log he hid behind. No wonder the ants were out in force. The log was so rotten he could practically see through it. *Nice protection.*

Minutes later, he eased his position a little, moving his leather-handled hunting knife around to a more comfortable position. The wide, heavy blade, honed to razor sharpness, was used for everything from shaving to cutting wood. Under his heavy buckskin shirt, sweat began running rivulets down his body and pooled in the small of his back. His mouth was cotton ball dry, and the canteen hanging on his saddle momentarily distracted him. But wishing wouldn't bring it to him.

The grazing horse snapped its head up, the reins snapping in the air. Raiders leaped out of the undergrowth where nothing had been but low bushes and rocks and a few forest fern—half-naked men burned brown by the sun. Disdaining the use of firearms, true to their newfound mantra, the raiders favored knives and clubs. The first raider came over the bushes in a magnificent leap, brandishing a knobby-ended club, screaming at the top of his lungs in primeval fury.

The blood-curdling cry abruptly cut short as Trent's thrown knife buried itself just under his breastbone with an audible thump. All that strength and stamina fell in a loose heap over the log. While the first raider was still sliding loosely to the ground, the second came bounding in.

Still on his knees behind the log and out of position to do anything else, he reluctantly palmed his gun and fired. The slug took the running man in the chest and the second and third rounds jerked him up on his toes in a frozen marionette pose, and then he slumped to the ground like a puppet with its strings cut.

Hearing a grunt from behind, he whirled in a flurry of leaves and sweat, partially evaded a swipe at his belly with a knife. He winced as the blade swept away and then blocked the overhand stab from the young raider. His Ruger went flying from his sweaty hands.

No one had taught the young raider how to fight with a knife, and he wasn't old enough to have learned from experience just how vulnerable you are with an overhand stab. He should have stayed with the sideways slashing that left the burning gash in Trent's side.

Even though he was just a boy, the raider didn't have any more time to learn. School was over and this was the final exam. There was a man-sized knife in the raider's hands, and a real sense of urgency driving Trent. If there were more raiders around, the sound of the shot would bring them in droves.

Stepping quickly inside the boy's downward swing, he caught his wrist and twisted the arm around and up behind his back. Heaving upward to dislocate the shoulder, the knife came away in Trent's hand. Hearing another raider coming from behind, he shoved the screaming boy away, slashing his throat left to right in a shower of blood. Pivoting on the follow-through, he faced the last raider amid the retching sounds of the boy behind him drowning in his own blood.

He crouched with his weight on the balls of his feet, lightly holding the captured knife with the cutting edge up and wishing he could dry his bloodied hands. He willed his breathing to slow, but his heart trip-hammered in his chest and wouldn't let him.

Except for the one shot, this encounter was relatively quiet. He wanted it to stay that way. Raiders rarely traveled in large groups, so there was a good chance this was all there were of this bunch. He glanced around for his own knife, but it was too far away, and he couldn't easily get to it. Looking quickly around for more raiders and not seeing any, he turned his steel-gray eyes on the man before him.

The last raider, standing well over six feet and heavily muscled, confident of his prowess, had seen Trent glance toward his own blade.

"Go ahead." The grinning raider made an expansive gesture toward the body holding Trent's knife. "I'll wait."

Trent, warily watching the big man, walked over and retrieved his knife, taking his time as he wiped the blood off on his victim's jeans. He stood drying his hands on his pant legs, waiting for the raider to make his move.

The man walked around flexing his muscles, putting on a show of loosening up, preening and showing off before his next kill. Who was he showing off for? That worried him a lot. The raider had crazy eyes that never left him, or the throwing arm that held the knife. One man had already been lost to his thrown knife.

Trent, seeing the rippling muscles and quick feet, knew he could not match this man on strength alone. He didn't intend to try.

"You're pretty good." The raider nodded at him. "You took care of them three boys real fast, but don't you get your hopes up. I'm better than them. I've killed lots of men better than you, and I'm going to gut you like a pig. You afraid of dying, boy?"

He smiled coldly at the raider. "You going to talk me to death?"

The smile faded from the raider's face. Cold eyes contemplated him for a moment before he replied. "No, boy. I'll use this." He raised his wide-bladed knife toward Trent.

With a shout, the raider lunged forward, the point of his knife held forward like a spear, hoping to impale Trent before he was set. He faded to one side, seeming to narrowly evade the lunge, but the move kept him close enough for his blade to flick out and nick the man's arm.

Blood welled from the small cut, and the raider sneered. "You'll have to do better than that, boy."

Furiously, the raider attacked him with broad sweeps and furious lunges, and the small clearing came alive with the sound of steel clashing against steel. Both men were breathing heavily and as if by common consent, stood apart a moment. He stood calm as he watched the man before him, a man whose arms and shoulders dripped with blood—a man who was tiring quickly because of what he considered insignificant blood loss.

Trent glanced cautiously from side to side. This encounter was taking too long. Every second he stayed in this place increased his danger. He needed to end this quickly.

With a curse, the raider renewed his attack, sweeping wide and slow with his blade and giving Trent the opportunity he needed. Slapping the raider's knife aside with his free hand, he came in under the outstretched arm and buried his knife in the man's belly. He pulled the blade up and over in a figure seven. Then, placing his left hand on the raider's chest pushed him away. It was short and brutal, leaving no chance for retaliation.

The man went backward and sat on the ground, vainly trying to hold his stomach together. He looked at Trent with shocked eyes as his heart pumped his life away through his fingers. The big raider tried to say something, but ran out of time. He fell gently sideways into the leaves, his final breath leaving in a long sigh rustling the grass.

Panting heavily, Trent quickly looked around him while retrieving his pistol and wiping dirt and leaves from the action. A flicker of movement away in the trees drew his momentary attention. He froze, watching and listening. *Nothing.* Slipping his pistol into its holster, he mounted the gelding, pulling the AK from its resting place as he settled in the saddle.

The encounter had left him unhurt, except for the shallow cut on his side. He glanced back at the raiders. Some might think him lucky, but he knew it was far more than that. He'd read about the ancient Berserkers who went wild in battle, bare-chested when others wore armor. This same anger came to him, even as a child, fighting with pointed sticks. Those sticks hurt and often he would lash out in fury, unleashed by a stinging wound from an opponent. Sometimes people called his fury bravery, but he could never accept that. Anyone who wasn't scared spitless in a fight was a fool.

He looked at the men who attacked him. Young, dirty, and getting no older. Looking at the youngest boy, he felt a wave of sadness wash over him. Even the young ones caught the raiding frenzy. He'd killed many times in the past, though never by choice. Always, the young ones bothered him the most.

With most of the country returned to a virgin wilderness, no one seemed to want to put out the effort to settle it again and restore some kind of order. He reasoned people could find something better to do with their time than prey on fellow survivors. But after the Fall and the collapse of civilization, the killing and fighting had become a way of life. *When would it end?*

He looked around the clearing one last time and suddenly felt tired. The one thing he wanted most from life was peace and quiet. With a sudden burst of clarity, he knew neither was likely. He was in the wrong business.

———

THE MAN STANDING at the window of the brick and wood-framed building was so large he blotted out the incoming sunlight. His mottled black and green uniform was severely pressed, the creases straight and sharp. Adorning his shoulders, the gold clusters of a colonel in the United States Army glittered in the light.

His unfocused gaze lingered on the street below, noting nothing in particular but acutely aware of all passing beneath him. It had become a ritual for him. Always hoping for change and never finding any.

The street below appeared to be controlled confusion at best. It was busy at this time of day, choked with horses, wagons, and an occasional motored vehicle whose type and looks were limited only by their owner's imagination.

"Look at all this, Fred." The Colonel spoke to his adjutant standing behind him. "When we first came here, this street was full of transport trucks and all-terrain armored vehicles. And tanks. Hell, we even had tanks. Our men controlled the town, the countryside, and all the roads in and out of camp. We were in total control. Now look at it. Horses and wagons, for God's sake. It looks like the 1800s all over again. The civilians are better armed than the soldiers. We are losing men from our units every day, and we don't know if they've been killed or just got tired of it all and walked away."

The lieutenant's voice was dangerously close to sounding bored, a dangerous situation because the Colonel would not tolerate boredom.

"How did we lose it, sir?"

Colonel Bonham did not turn away from the window. There wasn't any doubt of what his adjutant meant by the question. He and Lieutenant Fred Saints had discussed this subject many times before. It haunted the minds of those men left in power. Then...and now.

"It was easy, Fred. You know that. It was so damned easy and predictable. The American people just would *not* believe it was happening. Europe, sure, they are fighting all the time anyway. China, maybe so, with the billions of people they have, but not to us. Not to the good old U. S. of A. What has it been since the Fall? Twenty years?"

He didn't wait for a reply. "It started out like a bad sci-fi movie. The economy was a bust, businesses folding up by the thousands. The value of the dollar was dropping like a rock, and Congress didn't have a clue, Fred. Not one damned clue. They were so anal retentive, the whole bunch looked like a chocolate donut."

Smiling, Lieutenant Saints interjected, "And the rest of the world?"

"Jesus, what a mess." The Colonel didn't miss a beat. "Every country in the world got mad at somebody. Europe, Africa, Asia, South America—and we sent troops to all of them. Trying to police the world. What a waste. The United Nations was an impotent bunch of backsliders afraid of their own shadows."

"It was the anger, then?"

"Yeah, that and the floods and plague, and every other damned impossible thing that could go wrong."

"Speaking of which…"

The Colonel finally turned from the window. "Jesus, Fred. You've been waving that paper around all morning. I give up. I surrender. What is it? My discharge?"

The adjutant's haunted eyes held the colonels for a moment, ignoring the old joke usually resulting in a laugh. *Where would they go?*

"We got this by courier. There have been fresh outbreaks of plague back east. They say a lot of the water is bad. The whole thing may be starting over again, at least among all the people who drifted back to the big cities."

"Oh, that's just wonderful." The Colonel cast glittering eyes at the adjutant as he stomped toward a map on the wall. "I'm really glad you shared that with me, Fred."

"Sir, the dispatch says the GDCC is working on a vaccine."

"Right—the Government Disease Control Center." His voice was sarcastic. "With what, for Christ's sake? There haven't been any pharmaceuticals made in twenty years. What are they going to do, throw sticks at it? Bring in some witch doctor and scare it away? Cut open a chicken and look at the entrails? The scientific community never solved it twenty years ago, and they won't now.

"Look at this map, Lieutenant. This Ozark Project has to work. It may be our last hope. We're sitting right by one of the few safe areas left in the United States."

A pointer appeared magically in his hand, and he began to lecture his adjutant. "Do you see this section of the Mark Twain National Forest? It's a wilderness in there. Mountains and hills covered with forest and grass. The water is clear and cold, and the hills are full of all the game you want. Some settlements even have their own electricity. They run it from old gristmills on the rivers. It's just sitting there, ready and waiting for us. It's the best chance for our people to survive and start again. Over the last year, we've been gathering some of the best people we can find—the best minds, people with the talent to rebuild. We've got at least fifty families that we can put in there."

"Then what is the problem?"

The Colonel stood, lost in thought. Finally, he said, "Now that they are assembled, I'm afraid to send them in. I'm not too sure they would go anyway."

"Raiders."

Nodding, the Colonel turned back to the map and pointed to northern Arkansas. "The damned raiders. Big Springs is right here in the middle. It's a perfect spot for a settlement. They have their own water supply, electricity, and the works. They raided some hillbilly theme park nearby, Silver something or other, and from the old technology saved from the past, they now have leather working shops, bakeries, a place to cure meat, and enough farmland around close to raise wheat for bread."

He paused for a moment. "The area also has more raiders per square mile than a dog has fleas. The place is getting crowded."

"I'm surprised the raiders haven't taken everything over."

He grinned at his adjutant. "They have the same problem we do. Those red-necked hillbillies are stubborn as they come, and they don't move easy. Their places are isolated and hard to get to. And generally, they are well defended."

He pointed with his marker to the top of the map. "Jeremiah Starking has close to five hundred people here on the Upper Jacks Fork, northeast of Big Springs. Men, women, and kids. Maybe a hundred of them fighting men. He's ex-military and knows what he is doing. His people haven't turned raider yet, but they are not far from it. If anyone takes over, he would be the one. I don't think it will be long before he decides to move into the area. Trouble is, it won't support all of them and our people, too. He has some of his mercenaries in there now, stirring up things, seeing who's in charge and who they need to get rid of. From our last dispatch, we also know Pagan Reeves is there, and no one seems to know which side he is on. From the last report we received, Reeves was completely out of control."

"We have enough troops…"

"That is not an option, Lieutenant."

"What about the other Regional Commanders? Can't they send in troops?" Lieutenant Saint's voice was insistent.

He glared at his underling. "You still don't understand. We lost two patrols in the last month. Our soldiers aren't woodsmen. The raiders are. We are like the English going against the American Indian and Colonials. They are eating us alive in there. But what a company of soldiers can't do, might be done with just one man. If he's the right man."

"It would be suicide."

"Maybe." The Colonel's voice was soft. "But he might buy us enough time to get our men trained, though. If our man can keep them busy long enough."

Already guessing the answer, the adjutant sighed. "I suppose you have someone in mind?"

"Of course I do. John Trent. Do you remember the plan that passed through here last month about reinstating the United States Marshal Corp? I think we have our first recruit."

"But sir?" the adjutant said. "Begging your pardon, I know he was your son-in-law for a time, but do you think that's wise? Some people say he is worse than the raiders. Remember? Caplinger Mills two months ago? He killed four men and wounded two more. The people won't stand for it."

"Oh, they'll stand for it. They have to. No matter what you have heard, Lieutenant, John Trent is an honest man, and fair." His voice turned grim. "From the messages we receive, all that the people at Big Springs want is protection from the raiders. Well, they'll get their protection."

He turned his steely eyes on Saints. "You don't know what kind of man we're dealing with, do you?"

"You mean Trent. Guess not, sir, other than I think he is a cold-blooded killer."

"John Trent is a throwback. Somewhere in his genes are instincts and skills we couldn't begin to understand."

"You mean, like in the 1800s. Western frontier?"

"Not even close, lieutenant." He strode to the window again. "All these people you see out there? The traders, the soldiers, even the mercs and raiders to a certain degree, are still tied to civilization in some manner. As bad as the Fall was, there's still enough left of modern technology to shape us. We need things to survive, like tools, shelter, and survival gear. And we all need other people."

He paused a moment. "Trent doesn't need any of those things. You strip him naked and send him out in the wild, he'll come back fat and sassy and tear your heart out."

"I know he was married to your daughter, sir." Saints gave a derisive laugh. "I've even heard the rumor he doesn't like to fight."

He turned and looked directly at the lieutenant. "That's correct. He doesn't. Left alone, John Trent wouldn't harm a fly. He's a man who is very slow to anger. However, if given enough cause, the fire inside him shows no mercy. You have heard the expression, cold fire? When angered, he can become a killing machine and makes the old SEAL teams, Delta Force, or our Enforcers look like choirboys. He simply doesn't need us. He's totally self-reliant."

"So, you think Trent will get pushed too far by the raiders and take care of some of our problems."

"I'm counting on it." Colonel Frank Bonham chuckled mirthlessly. "The town of Big Springs wants a company of soldiers. What they'll get is one man. They'll get John Trent."

"Well then, if all you say is true, God help them." The adjutant was shaking his head ruefully.

Colonel Bonham snapped his head around and stared at his assistant. "No. God help the raiders."

————

THE WIND through the trees was a whispering rustle as the man on the roan gelding gazed across the hills making up the Ozark Mountains in southern Missouri. The nearer hills were sharp in the morning light, a mural etched in different shades of green and brown, broken by gray limestone outcroppings, cliff faces, and an occasional abandoned farmhouse. Dark, successive hills gradually faded away in the haze and mist of the morning. The fresh breeze would soon push away the haze, revealing deep valleys and high mountainous hills choked with so much scrub brush and vegetation it was nearly impossible to pass through unless you knew the way. The oak and maple trees spread a canopy over the forest, while pine and cedar tried to soak up what sunlight passed through the leaves above.

John Trent felt at peace with himself as he relaxed in the saddle, sitting well back from the cliff face, and close under the shade of an old, gnarled oak. He idly reached out and touched the dark, crusty bark, feeling its texture through fingers as hardened as the bark, and wondered how many of nature's denizens made their home in this one old tree. The tree had taken all the punishment time could give it—its bark twisted and hardened by the forces of nature, yet still keeping its uniformity in shape and size. For over a hundred years, judging by its size, the oak had stood, benignly watching the parade of humanity pass through these hills. Of course, there wasn't much of a parade anymore. Nature had taken care of that.

He felt an affinity for the oak, for his body, too, had stood the test of time, hardened and tempered by the fires of survival until he was as much a product of nature as the oak. The difference was...he could feel, and see, and because of those things...know regret. The oak would never feel regret, or get tired of its life. He envied the oak for that simplicity.

Trent knew the tiredness often slumping his shoulders wasn't physical. Mostly, it was a mental state. On occasion, in somber moments of reflection, he marveled at the senselessness of what the world had become. He could feel the emotions coming up in him, a gusher that, even when capped, still let rivulets escape. It was like trying to stop the leaks in a dam with your fingers. At some point, you will run out of fingers.

For the most part, he understood how the raiders felt, which was one thing separating him from his peers. The other scouts and couriers in the Combined Armed Forces, USA, just reacted, without caring, to whatever happened to be going on at the moment. The raider did not feel despair or remorse of any kind. They harbored an impotent anger at the world for becoming such a place. Anger, because the world had lost so much. Anger, because death seemed to be the easy, if not only, way out. In death, you aren't hungry, or cold, or so damned tired you can't stand up. In death, you aren't afraid to close your eyes at night to rest, fearing some other raider who is just as scared and cold as you, may sneak up and cut your throat for the blanket you're wrapped up in. Raider. The very word brought fear in the eyes of the Army and settlement people alike. Their mantra was simple. No plans, just live for the day. Anyone not in your group is an enemy. Do not trust anyone, and never...ever...show weakness.

John had been on the fringes of this for years. He had joined the Army at the age of seventeen. Like so many people, all he wanted was the guarantee of a place to sleep, and food to eat. He got his wish. But the price he paid was involvement in more border wars and peace-keeping missions than he cared to think about.

The remarkable event known as the Fall had started years before, like a slow growing cancer, and then spread like wildfire through the country. No one knew what started the plague, or cared. He didn't want to know who to hate. It didn't matter anymore. Back east, they were slowly rebuilding. West of the Mississippi River, however, the land was lawless and brutal. Death could come at any moment...and often did.

He was a man who'd been around and at thirty-one, was already older than the new adjusted life span of the American male. Riding dispatch for the Provisional Government, mainly between Army posts, he could do what he did best. Couriers were about the only means of communication left for the Army, and it took a skilled woodsman to navigate the forests, which were infested with raiders just waiting to kill a lone traveler for whatever he was carrying, especially weapons.

Rule one: Remain unseen and cover a lot of ground.

Rule two: Never forget rule one.

He realized he had a natural ability, born in the gene pool of ancestors he never knew. As a child, he lived close to the woods and would always retreat to the cool confines of the forest whenever he needed to get away. Once in the Combined Forces, all his assignments had been in the jungles of Central America and South America.

Now, on the new frontier of his own country, he rarely ventured into the settlements and left the Army camps he had to visit as quickly as possible. But trouble was always near. No one could avoid it entirely. Lately, he didn't try as much to avoid trouble. It seemed like, at some inner level, he was beginning to welcome it. Some perverse part of him knew just how good he was, and just how much better than most others at the business of survival. He had eye-hand coordination that dazzled ordinary men. And worst of all, he could feel himself becoming more callous to death and suffering every day.

At least that is how it had been until two weeks ago. Two weeks ago, he had been in Pine Bluff...two weeks ago, he had killed a man. As he scanned the forest around him, Trent's mind pushed and pulled at the scab of memory that itched and just wouldn't go away.

———

YEARS AGO, one of his instructors had talked to Trent about killing. A soldier expects to have to kill. It's their business. They should not expect anything else. Yet, even the most callous of soldiers will one day find himself thinking too much about death and his part in administering it. The instructor gave a strong warning.

"It's not the quantity...it's the quality. Some people just need killing. You cannot reason with them, and you sure as hell can't change them. They are rotten to the core, so you go after them for God and country or any other reason that floats your boat. When they are dead—you toss them aside with the rest of the garbage, because that is what they are. Problem is, if you are good, it starts getting easy. The killing becomes automatic, and you find yourself taking less and less time to decide. Then, one day you will kill someone of whom you aren't sure. You start doubting and hesitating. All the black and white in your world turns to gray. You start second-guessing your-self, and when that happens, it's time to get out. Other-wise, you die. Probably killed by the same people you were trying to protect."

That particular day two weeks ago started innocently enough. He rode into a little jerkwater town, having about four buildings with three of them falling down, two jumps ahead of a bunch of raiders. He didn't know if they were true raider, or just a bunch of 'good ole boys' out to hoorah the stranger out of their neck of the woods. Both scenarios were entirely possible. About twenty of them had come bursting out of a draw next to the road where he was riding, half of them on foot, the rest on horses, screaming and yelling.

He was already hot and tired and more than just a little cranky, so instead of running, he pulled his old AK47 out and laid ten rounds into the asphalt in front of them. The 7.62mm bullets had shattered on the pave-ment, and the ricochets took out the knees of some of the horses. The resulting bedlam and confusion had allowed Trent to get ahead of them.

Coming into the town, it reminded him of a picture

postcard he'd seen once. The caption was, "How do you know you're in the Ozarks? If when someone's front porch falls in...it kills more than twenty dogs." This town seemed to have more dogs than people. It's always good to know where you are.

Pulling up in front of what he guessed would pass for a saloon, he entered and pushed his way up to the bar.

"Got anything cool?" he asked.

Cool seemed to be a matter of interpretation. Cool was the stare he got from the man behind the planks of wood they were using for a counter.

"All right." Trent shrugged, conceding the point. "Do you have anything to drink?"

Anything turned out to be a glass of bust-head moonshine, which threatened to rip the hair right off his head. He held the glass gingerly up to the dust-filtered sunlight coming in through the door, then gently set it down on the counter as if he were afraid it would explode.

"Man, that corn is a little green."

The natural reserve of the hill people broke a little, and the barman had grinned and said plaintively, "Been aged to perfection. Almost a week."

Trent, his eyes still watering from the drink, heard a chair scrape back on the floor. He turned to see a man standing in the corner of the room, legs spread, his right hand near his weapon. The table he had backed away from held three more men, still holding cards and looking like they wished they had business somewhere else.

"C'mon, Lenny, leave the man alone," one of the men said. "I got a good hand goin' here."

Lenny's face was in shadow, but Trent could plainly see his sidearm. It was an automatic, maybe a Browning or Colt, slung low in a plastic holster like the old SWAT teams used to wear. Fast draw artist? Gunman? Nut case? Who the hell knew?

All this flashed through his mind in the few seconds it took the wanna-be bad man to think of something appropriate to say.

"You." Lenny's voice was loud in the small room. "In the buckskins. You one of them Army scouts we been hearing about?"

Trent looked at him for a moment and then said neutrally, "I am a courier for the Army. I'm also tired, thirsty, and not looking for trouble." It was in his mind to turn back to the bar and ignore the trouble hunter. But it wasn't to be...

The man's hand was resting on the butt of his pistol. When his hand moved, Trent shot him in the chest. The mushrooming bullet left a conical pattern of blood on the wall behind him—the half-pulled pistol fell to the floor, followed closely by the man.

The bystanders in the bar were shocked into silence. No one really liked Lenny, but he was one of their own, and he was down on the floor. Sure, he was a trouble hunter. He had even killed several raiders who had come to town hunting trouble.

The eyes of the men in the bar finally moved away from the body on the floor. All eyes were riveted on Trent, standing by the bar. One second he was standing there, the next he was holding a smoking revolver. No one saw him draw; it was that fast. Even the bartender had missed it.

He walked up to the man he'd shot. There wasn't any doubt the man would die. He knew where he'd aimed. Looking down, he was shocked at the age of the man.

Man? A boy...and he was bubbling his life out of a small hole just under his left nipple. An older man kneeling by the boy looked accusingly at Trent.

The man's voice was low and ponderous. "You didn't have to kill him."

The comment startled him. In his mind, there wasn't a choice. "He started to draw his gun." Even to him, it sounded lame and hollow. "He would have killed me if I hadn't stopped him."

"He's just a kid, and you're a soldier. You could have wounded him if you had wanted to."

And there it was. Standing there, watching the boy vainly rolling his stomach, drowning in his own blood as he tried to fill his lungs with air, Trent's shoulders slumped. Could he have simply wounded the boy? The question kept rolling around in his head. The answer was...no. But it had never occurred to him. Why?

The men in the saloon turned their backs on him and left him standing alone in the middle of the floor. Finally, he walked out to his horse, mounted up, and started a slow walk out of town. As he left, he heard a woman screaming. Loved one? Mother? He didn't know.

Two weeks later...he could still hear her screaming.

———

TRENT SHOOK HIS HEAD, clearing out the cobwebs of memories, and silently eased his tall frame to a more comfortable position in the saddle, looping one leg around the horn. He wore desert-style moccasins that covered his legs from foot to knee. Cut out from the neck of an old brindle bull, the soles were made of several layers of hide sewn together. The leggings covered him up to his knees, adding protection against the rigors of the trail, where it seemed every bush had a thorn on it, just waiting to tear up anything passing by. He thoughtfully rubbed smooth a scratch on the leather, thinking of the bull.

That old bull had almost cost Trent his life. He came up on it in the close confines of a brush-lined trail, deep in the southern Missouri hills. The bull was a cross of Texas Longhorn, Brangus, and an unadulterated anger at the world. His six-foot spread of razor-sharp horns had been catching in the brush along the trail, the heel flies had found him about an hour back, and the mud hole he wanted to roll in, to get rid of the flies, was full of wild pigs. Even a macho Longhorn bull is too smart to mess with a bunch of razorbacks.

When they met, the trail was such that there was no turning around for either man or beast, and the last bullet from Trent's revolver had finally stopped the bull's charge right in front of his horse's nose. At that point, he seriously thought of switching his pistol to an autoloader that would hold rounds.

He skinned the animal and spent a few days curing some of the better portions of the meat. It was hard and stringy, not much better than the hide, but it was food.

———

PUSHING his brown Bushman's hat back on his head, Trent enjoyed the brief coolness as the sweat trapped by his hatband gave up its moisture to the breeze. His face was smooth and browned by the sun; his gray eyes were always searching and cataloging everything around him. The eyes were never still, and the edges were crinkled into crow's feet from squinting against the sun. A man of infinite patience, he slowly scanned the country, looking for signs of other men. For in this time and place, the most dangerous animal in the forest was man.

As he sat, resting his horse and enjoying the shade, his mind worked on two levels. His subconscious mind was busy with the minute-by-minute evaluation of possible danger. Having an acute sixth sense, he was barely aware on a surface level of all this. It was simply that, being raised in the forest, he was a part of the forest...its every sound and breath, and he was *of* the forest as much as any animal that lived there. It was his home.

Movement across the valley caught his attention. His eyes narrowed as he sat motionless in the saddle, his gaze focusing on a small area of the forest. Without taking his eyes from the place he had seen movement, he reached back and took a small pair of binoculars from his pouch. They were a two-toned green in mottled design and rubberized to keep the weather out. At least, that is what the instructions said. He wanted them because the rubber coating would keep the glasses from making noise in his pack.

All his equipment was like that. A clink or rattle at the wrong time could spell disaster on the trail.

Moving the small wheel between the barrels of the glass, he focused in on the spot of movement, seeing several buzzards wheeling in formation over something, coming lower with each circle. Something had scared them up, and now they were settling down again.

Returning the glasses to their pouch, he settled his hat and clucked at the horse to get him moving. The roan gelding had been with him for several seasons and seemed to know his every mood and whim. Tough and mean, the horse was a lot of trouble in the mornings, liking to buck and twist, trying to unseat his rider. The horse was a fighter and stayer, though, which meant more to him than a few minor altercations every morning.

He knew he had to see what attracted the buzzard's attention. There were too many birds for it to be a small animal. It could be something large, like a dead cow or horse, maybe a deer...or it could be like the Army patrol he had found a few weeks before, shot to rag dolls and scattered along the trail like so much trash along the road.

He couldn't see the buzzards—didn't need to. Deep in his belly, a cold knot was forming, and he felt that oppressive feeling coming, like the low clouds of a summer storm. He didn't know what he would find, but his gut told him it would be bad. Really bad.

TWO

TRENT PULLED up to give his horse and himself another breather. He stopped to rest every fifteen minutes because of the route he traveled. The mountainous terrain of southern Missouri did not lend itself to fast-paced travel, especially if you wandered off the main roads and trails, and he hardly ever traveled the main trails.

They'd just traversed the valley the hard way, picking their way in a zigzag pattern down the mountain and up the side of the next, and finally come to the area where he saw the buzzards. The air was hot and sticky, with hardly a breeze fanning the trees. The flies found his sweaty horse a few miles back, following in a swarm around horse and rider. Rippling its skin and swatting its tail, the gelding was skittish and irritable. The horse wanted nothing more than a good roll in the dust, but he held him in with a firm hand on the reins, patting his shoulders and making small sounds to comfort him.

When the gelding finally settled down, he returned

his steady gaze to the open glade in the forest ahead. Starting to nudge the horse forward, he stopped abruptly.

He couldn't explain it to anyone if he tried. Somewhere on a subconscious level, bells were ringing and clanging like dueling Methodist and Lutheran church belfries on Sunday morning. There was something ahead. It was a tangible force, an unknown presence. He could feel it, nearly taste it, and because of it, every pore of his body screamed caution. He was not about to move. Not yet. Not until he knew.

As long as they didn't move, he and his horse would be nearly invisible to anyone watching the area. That is, if his horse had not already given them away by prancing around.

A flurry of wings beating the ground and a raucous squawking from the turkey buzzards brought a momentary scrutiny. Their sudden flight caused his hand to sweep toward the revolver at his waist and as quickly come to rest on his thigh. The buzzards were skittish, too. Restless. And even though they had to be the ugliest birds in creation, he still trusted their senses over his own.

Still and silent, the man and horse seemed to be made of stone. His eyes relentlessly searched the forest, all his senses keyed to the slightest thing out of the ordinary, like a sound or a shadow in the wrong place. Anything. Something to justify the feeling he had.

And it remained with him, covering him like a shroud over a casket. Making a small sound of exasperation, he scanned the clearing one more time. Nothing. It was just another bald spot in the forest. Time to move.

He sat at the edge of a small clearing, brush and small trees nearly obscuring his horse. Quietly, he dismounted, taking the AK from its scabbard on his way down, not liking even the small noise it made leaving the scabbard. The thirty-round clip was full, but the chamber was empty. He didn't want to risk pulling back the charging handle to load it. Noise carries well in the forest, especially sharp, metallic noises.

He let his breath out slowly. It was too quiet. The silence of the forest was so loud it made the hair stand up on the back of his neck. No birds were singing, no insects buzzing, even the breeze seemed to hesitate, waiting for permission to move, waiting to see what would happen. The heat was stifling, even in the shady confines of the trees. He stood in one place for over ten minutes. In a country filled with raiders who preyed on settlers and Army patrols alike, it didn't pay to be in a hurry. Army dispatches could wait, and he hadn't lost anything on the other side of that clearing.

For just a moment, he could feel a presence ahead of him, something real and tangible...and then it was gone, leaving him with an unfathomable feeling of relief. Not once did he doubt what he felt. A mystical concept to most people, something you had to feel to understand. The sixth sense of any good woodsman was a phenomenon he couldn't begin to explain.

Finally, the blanket of silence lifted like fog leaving the ground and the small creatures of the forest took up their daily business. A thrush called inquiringly for its mate, a tree frog began a perfect insect imitation, and a blue jay looked disgustedly down at a beetle it had just dropped on the ground. The forest finally gave up a small breeze, whispering through the pines with a lonely sigh and cooling his sweaty brow.

The clearing was about a hundred feet across,

surrounded by tall trees keeping half of the open space always in shadow. Outcroppings of rocks dotted the glade, and the native grass grew short in places, evidence of the thousands of deer living in the forest.

The girl's body lay near the center of the clearing, the afternoon sun sending its creeping shadows slowly around the edges, never to touch the middle. He stopped a few feet from her. Usually callous at the face of death, today his feelings started at nausea and then gave way to dull, throbbing anger. He stood for a moment, shoving down the bile rising to find release, and filed the anger away for a more useful time. Forcing his eyes away from the body, he took in the surrounding area. He'd seen hundreds of dead bodies, but never anything like this. No one could be ready for this.

Even through the assault on his senses, he could not shake the feeling someone was watching him. And with that thought, he deliberately pulled back the charging handle on the AK, letting it go with a loud clacking sound as the first bullet was chambered. Noise be damned. If someone was watching, let it be a warning.

He turned from scrutinizing the forest and forced himself to contemplate the body. Having been a woodsman since childhood, he could read the message on the forest floor as easily as someone else could read a book. It's just a matter of understanding what you see.

But there wasn't much to see. No tracks or anything to give a clue about who did this. Nearby was a branch, presumably used to rough up the grass, getting rid of tracks and indentations. The leaves on the branch were wilted and wrinkled but still had green color. *Today then. Early.*

Finally, when he'd looked at everything he could see

from his position, he reluctantly walked closer to the body. *Hours—no more.* The buzzards circling above hadn't worked on her yet, nor had small scavengers done their damage.

He took in the smooth features of the girl's face, the luxurious canopy of hair, half-open blue eyes staring fixedly at the sky. She'd once been a beautiful girl, but death robbed her of that...especially this kind of death. Now, she was just one more naked piece of garbage left on mankind's doorstep, with stark horror stamped on her face.

Trent tried to force himself to be objective. He suppressed his anger earlier. Now it was flowing again and quickly turning into resolution. *The animal that would do this to anyone, but especially a girl...I'm going to find.* He paused long enough to scan the tree line again. *I will find you.*

The girl was spread-eagled on the grass. From the cuts and burns on her wrists and ankles, he knew she'd been restrained, her arms and legs tied to short stakes driven into the ground. The holes in the ground would be about the size for tent stakes, as you could find in abandoned hardware stores or could make yourself. Her clothing, cut from her with a knife after someone staked her down, remained under her, catching the pooling blood turned black and covered with ants.

That wasn't all the work done with the knife. The sharply defined wounds on her body were distinct and sharp, her face covered in blood, brown hair matted with leaves and dirt. The girl's breasts had been sliced open with x's, and her nipples were gone. Her stomach, cut open and pulled apart, was such a mess he couldn't tell about other damage. Her legs were scratched and bloody, with much of her brown pubic hair sliced away.

Taking a huge breath and starting with the body as the center of his search, he walked around the clearing in ever-widening circles. As he walked, he absentmindedly swore in a low monotone voice dripping with anger and loathing. He'd seen dead people before, had killed more than he liked to think about, all in the name of survival. Neither the smell nor the visage of death was new to him. He looked back at the girl lying on the grass. *Nothing like this. Never anything like this.*

"Well, hell." His soft curse was a short epitaph of emotion and feeling. No one deserved to die like this. He could see where the pieces of rope tying her to the stakes had cut into her arms. The girl had possessed spirit. She had fought...fought hard. Looking at her, he was obsessed with the "why" of the killing. Why this way? Why so brutal? Revenge? Maybe. Doubtful. Rape? It happens. But mutilate the girl afterward? No. Even a raider wouldn't do that. Raiders would want to save her for later.

So, this wasn't raiders out on a killing spree. Although the wounds would have been terribly painful, they did not coincide with any kind of torture he'd read about. He searched his memory, thinking of all the men, or women for that matter, that he knew. He searched for anything to help him understand. Finally, he admitted to himself that he didn't have a clue—and that was a place he didn't like to be.

He often moved within the raider camps. They knew he was no threat to them, understanding that he didn't judge them. Raiders who knew him generally wouldn't bother him, and he responded in kind. But this killing didn't make any kind of sense.

Raiders killed in anger. They killed to protect hunting rights, often laying claim to a certain section of country. Some of the wilder ones he knew would kill just for the sheer joy of battle, but that same battle would involve another man and be in a stand-up fight. Who would do this?

This killing was different, and that difference chilled him. It was not a killing over clean water, or a place to sleep, or something to eat. Someone had done this for the sheer joy of killing. From this perspective, an inkling of understanding dawned on him, and he looked at the body again. All the wounds were methodical and precise. If there was anger here, it didn't show in the way the girl was killed. At least, nothing showed on the surface. He didn't see mad slashing or stab wounds. One thing he suspected. Whoever did this...liked it. And liked it a lot.

Trent stopped by the branch used as a broom to rough up the grass. He squatted on his heels and looked closely at the ground. Whoever did this tried to brush out their tracks, sweeping the branch across the grass and dirt until they came close to an outcropping of limestone leading into the forest. He assumed that would be the killer's escape route. Slowly and methodically, he looked for signs, and finally, close to the first rock, found the only clue he was to find. He could see a smooth, rounded impression in the dirt that could be a heel print. Moccasins? Trent put his foot beside the print. The print was smaller than his. Not much, but it was a start.

Suddenly, a cold chill swept over him. The warning bells he had been ignoring were clamoring inside his head again. He wasn't alone.

THREE

TRENT STRAIGHTENED and turned slowly to see a tall, willowy woman standing at the edge of the forest. Her dark blond hair was stuffed up under a green camouflaged field hat, and the coldest blue eyes he had ever seen were staring, unblinking, down the barrel of her assault rifle. Her gaze didn't waver a fraction, and a quick glance told him the safety was down and off. The black bore of the barrel looked large enough to ride through with his hat on.

She was nearly as tall as he, and he stood over six feet. Blond hair, tied in a ponytail that he judged would fall to her waist when let loose. The first few buttons on her thin, white cotton blouse were undone, because of the heat, he guessed, and the action of aiming the rifle had parted the front so he could see the sides of her breasts—her deeply tanned throat in startling contrast to the white skin beneath.

Her pants were homemade buckskin, like his, but hers were tighter and filled out differently. How she filled them out made him sweat. Girls you wanted to take a chance with were few and far between, and it'd been a while.

Leather boots covered her feet. *Sensible.* And a long-bladed knife hung from a belt strapped around her waist. *Dangerous.*

When he finally raised his eyes from her body to her face, her eyes were mocking him.

"Sure took you a long time to get to my face." Her voice was low and censuring, seeming to chide him for the trip.

"I take my time with beautiful things."

They stood watching each other, both slightly off balance in their positions. The seconds stretched out as their gaze locked together. The gray eyes of the man held tight to the robin's egg blue of the girl, sinking deeper and deeper until they both ached to blink.

He saw her come to a decision, and her voice hardened. "Drop the rifle."

It was gamble time. She didn't look like a killer. "Can't do that." He saw the muzzle shift a fraction, but the sonic 'whap' of the bullet passing his ear still made him flinch. The muzzle flash didn't distract him from watching the ejected casing as it made a slow, glittering, arch in the sunlight, then disappeared into the tall grass. His heart tripped into high gear as his ears rang. *Maybe he wouldn't need to hear anything until tomorrow. Damn, that hurt.*

Their gaze still met over the sights of her gun, holding steady with each other as he weighed his options. Slowly, one of her eyebrows arched, and he saw resolution come into her eyes.

He bent over slowly and placed the rifle on the ground. She followed his movement with the barrel of her gun and he almost smiled. When he straightened, she was slow to follow with the rifle. The split second cost her. Her muzzle pointed down, and his pistol lined up with her belly.

"How in hell...?" She was startled, but the rifle was coming up.

"Don't," Trent interjected quickly to stop her. He held his hand palm out to her. "I don't think either of us wants to be shot today."

"You got that right." Her answer was tight-lipped and unafraid.

After a moment, she casually tilted her rifle and leaned it on her shoulder, muzzle pointing up and backward. The position did not fool him. She could still bring the rifle to bear very quickly. This girl had been around the block a few times. Her glance shifted to the body she could barely see, a few feet behind Trent. "Your kill?"

He shook his head disgustedly. "Not hardly."

"Do you mind if I take a look?" She stood waiting for a sign from him and looked wound up tight as a spring.

"Can we call a truce first?"

She didn't answer, looking instead at the barrel of the gun still lined on her belly. Looking back up at him, she raised her eyebrows in an unspoken question.

Suddenly realizing he still had a gun on her, he abruptly rocked back the revolver, letting the hammer down in the process, and smoothly slipped the gun into its oiled holster. The quickness of his hands weren't lost on her.

"I saw the birds." The low contralto voice came out and softly caressed his ears.

He knew she saw him glance toward the forest, then back at her. What was she doing here?

The girl still had not moved. "What happened here?"

He glanced back at the grotesquely displayed body. Now that another woman was present, he was uncomfortable at the victim's nakedness and wanted to cover her.

"Woman died."

She nodded her head toward the clearing. "I saw you looking around. Did you find any sign?"

He rubbed his forehead with the back of his hand and knew his frustration was showing. "Not much to see. Whoever it was, wiped their tracks clean and didn't leave so much as a bent twig."

"Do you mind if *I* take a look around?" The girl's voice emphasized the I.

He realized she didn't trust him, and he couldn't blame her.

The tall girl looked steadily at him for a moment. Her gaze openly searched his face and took in the rest of him in a long, slow glance. It was his turn to feel uncomfortable under her scrutiny.

"You're one of Colonel Bonham's couriers." It was a statement rather than a question.

He inclined his head slightly and gave her a grudging smile. "Good guess."

The girl walked around him, keeping some distance between them. Nearing the body, she got her first real look. "Jesus God."

Her hand came up to her mouth, and she turned away for a moment. A deep shuddering breath, then a couple more, and he could see the strength coming into her. He watched her fight down the horror and revulsion. She straightened, and from a side view, he could see firmness come into her face.

"You might have warned me."

As he walked silently up to her, he could see the start of tears in her eyes, tears denied with a violent shake of her head. "I wanted to see how you reacted. Women can kill as easily as men. Do you know her?"

Startled, realizing how close they were, she stepped away from him. "Yeah, I know her."

"Where is she from?"

She looked at him, and for a moment, he didn't know if she'd answer. "Big Springs, over east of here."

"Who was she?"

The answers came easier now. "We called her Markie...I don't remember a last name."

"Do you know what she was doing out here?" He paused, putting an indictment into the next word. "Alone?"

"Same as me." Her gaze was steady on his.

This is like pulling teeth. "I was wondering about that, too. You being alone, I mean."

She looked like she'd finally had enough. "You writin' a book? What difference does it make to you?"

He shrugged his shoulders. "Curious, is all. I don't like finding girls staked out on the ground like this."

As he started toward his horse for a shovel, the girl called to him. "You got a name, or will 'hey you' be all right?"

"Trent. John Trent."

He watched as the girl took a half step backward, and the barrel of the rifle completed a half-circle as the bottom grip of the gun slapped into her palm. A slick, practiced move, and somehow he knew it would be. "I've heard of you."

———

INDEED, she had. The exploits of John Trent were known around campfires and kitchens and other gathering places where men and women congregated to talk of their new world. Stories of Trent, fired across tables, rolled about the stables, embellished and memorized by the people on this new frontier.

Fascinated, she tried to match up the man with the stories she had heard. The stories were of a brutal fighter, giving no quarter to anyone. Something in the picture he presented was wrong, but she couldn't quite put her finger on it. The size was right, and he certainly looked tough enough. The man she'd heard about was supposed to be a cold-eyed character that would as soon kill you as look at you. An ex-soldier, rumored to be a sometime mercenary, expert with knife or gun, and known up and down the new frontier as a bad man to tangle with.

Trent interrupted her thoughts. "If you have heard of me, you should know I wouldn't do something like this."

She conceded the point with a short nod. "It explains something, though."

He looked at her expectantly.

Her lips curled in a wry smile. "Tells me where that pistol came from in such a hurry."

———

HE WAS UNROLLING a pack from his horse, looking for a small fold-up shovel, when she came up to him. He had been watching her and was grudgingly impressed by the way she handled herself. He could not hear her walking around. She kind of toed in and glided, taking care where she walked, smooth and easy. He raised his eyebrows, asking a silent question.

"You were right." Her face was deadpanning it. "She's dead."

His eyes raked her with silent reproach, even as he realized her stab at humor was her way of handling the morbid situation. It seemed funny to him, now that she knew who he was, she seemed to be more trusting.

Finally...

"Markie and I were on our way to see the Army at base camp. Sometimes we go there and pick up supplies we can't find in the deserted towns. Especially ammo. After the Army swept the area clean a few years ago, some things get kind of scarce. I didn't know Markie very well, and yesterday she just took off on her own. Said she would see me at the Army camp."

"You didn't have any men to send?"

He knew at once that he'd said the wrong thing. The soft blue eyes turned to flint and ice.

"Look, Mr. Army Courier. I was born and raised in these woods. You won't find anyone better, and I surely don't need to be a man to find my way around."

"This Markie, was she born and raised in the woods, too?" When he saw her about to blow up, he sidetracked her with another question. "When I had the drop on you, you were still going to try and shoot me. Why'd you stop?"

She looked at him seriously for a moment. "I'm not so young and stupid that I don't know what can happen to women out here. I decided a long time ago that I would rather die. It's that simple."

"But then, you didn't."

She shrugged. "I also trust my own judgment. You are no killer—at least, not that way."

———

IT WAS ABOUT AN HOUR LATER, and he'd just finished digging the grave. He didn't know why, but he dug it extra deep to keep varmints from uncovering her. After being used so badly she deserved at least this small favor.

They didn't speak as he rolled her in a spare blanket. He thought they were lucky. The body hadn't started to bloat much. He had buried far worse, and it was always a thankless job.

Together they picked the blanket up by both ends and carried the body to the grave.

After they filled the grave and packed the dirt on top, he turned to the girl.

"Do you know any words to say?"

She looked at him quizzically, surprised he had thought of it, and then nodded her assent. They bowed their heads.

Her voice was quiet and subdued. "Lord, we didn't know this woman much. I expect you do. She didn't deserve any of this. Take good care of her." She hesitated a little and anger seeped into her voice. "And take care of the bastard that did this to her. Amen."

She looked at him for approval, got it with a nod, and began gathering up her gear.

He was naked to the waist, sweating in the heat coming with the late afternoon sun, as he packed away his shovel. His shirt was draped over the pommel of the saddle, and his muscles rippled across his chest and arms as he tightened the girth and made sure all the straps were tight on his packs.

"You're wounded."

He glanced down at his side, shrugging. "Just a cut. Had a little set-to with some raiders."

The girl glanced apprehensively around the clearing before bringing her gaze back to him. "We should be moving, then. They may have followed you."

"No. They won't. Not those, anyway." He paused a moment. "I'm assuming this Markie had a horse? Maybe a rifle of some kind...supplies?"

"She rode a small dappled gray mare, gentle as can be. Had a nice rifle though...an AR-15 semi. Not too many of those around anymore. Most weren't very good quality to start with."

He nodded. "I'll be on the lookout for the horse. Suppose I could know your name?" His soft voice and change of subject seemed to startle her a moment.

She smiled at him, mocking him with her gaze because he hadn't thought of asking before. "My name is Katie Stephens. If you make it to base camp, look me up. I'll be around for a few days. Or, if your dispatches take you through Big Springs...?"

"Katie. Short for Katherine?"

Giving him a wary glance, she replied, "No one calls me Katherine but people very close to me."

"But I like Katherine." Before she could reply, he deliberately changed the subject. "I'll ask again, and this time I want an answer. This girl we just buried. She was born and raised in the woods, too?"

Katie was momentarily flustered by the change of subject. "Yeah. Markie was even better in the woods than me."

"Really? Well, she wasn't near good enough. You think about that, Katherine Stephens."

She searched his eyes a moment before giving a reply. "Point taken. See you around."

"It might be better if we travel together." His hand on her arm was gentle, and she easily shrugged out of it.

"I better go on alone." Her gaze held his, wavered a moment, then the coolness came, and she turned away.

"Katherine?"

Her eyes came to his again, blue against gray. Blue fire against tempered steel.

"He's still out there."

A cold chill seemed to make her shiver. "I know. But I'm not anything like Markie." Her voice carried quietly to him. "I won't end up like her. She suddenly turned at the edge of the clearing. "I have it."

"What?"

"It's the eyes. Your eyes are too soft for the things you do." She stood looking at him with a satisfied smile.

His reply was puzzled. "Translation?"

"It means some girl might have a chance of sweeping you off your feet." It was a lighthearted statement, but the question was there in her eyes.

He smiled at her and said grudgingly, "Maybe so."

Trent stood in the clearing after she left, thinking about what she'd said about being different from the dead girl. "I hope you are right, Katherine. I sure as hell hope you're right."

She'd gone into the dense thicket next to the clearing. He heard her patting her horse, then the creak of a saddle as she mounted. Then she was gone, making no more sound than yesterday's dreams.

He stood, looking up the mountain. Whoever had

killed the girl in the clearing was, indeed, still out there. He could feel it. Like a vein throbbing in his head, he could still feel the killer's presence. The thought came to him that, just maybe, this killing was not the first or last, for the assailant. The method looked like some kind of ritual. And rituals are something you do over and over.

Trent knew he would have to report the killing to the Colonel. Maybe they would send a patrol out. *Then again, maybe not. And where?* What's one more dead body in the wake of the millions gone before?

He shook himself to free his mind of the problem. Time to quit daydreaming and deliver the dispatches. The trail ahead was dangerous enough without him being preoccupied with something else, but he couldn't get the picture of the mutilated girl out of his mind. He'd like to get his hands on whoever did this. Just for a little while...

He pointed his horse's head toward the Army camp. He'd pick up Katherine's trail and follow her into camp. Afterward, he had a job to do. He'd be coming back.

"No, Katherine, you won't end up like that."

———

THE WATCHER STOOD *amid the trees, silent and brooding. Far below, barely visible in the subdued light, his latest offering lay supplicating the heavens. Before the cleansing carrion birds could do their work, he saw them suddenly take wing in a flurry of dust and feathers. His eyes narrowed as he took in the scene below. What scared them away? A slight movement at the edge of the clearing drew his attention. He watched with knowing satisfaction as the man eased into the clearing, trusting nothing as he gazed around him. Too far away to see facial expression, he was immediately aware when the man in the clearing accepted what had happened to the girl. He could tell by body language alone. He could feel the rage emanating from the man and suppressed the urge to run and hide as the man in buckskins suddenly turned and looked up the mountain. Seemingly, right at him. Ah, he's good. He feels. It's proper that this man should find this latest offering. After all, what good is a sacrifice—if no one sees it?*

———

TRENT WAS STILL two days from base camp when he cut Katherine's trail again. She'd lost him the day before, but knowing her ultimate destination, he just continued toward the Army camp.

Now he followed a small tributary that flowed toward the Upper Jacks Fork on the Currant River. The small stream kept ducking down into the limestone of the mountain and then reappearing farther along. As with most of this area in Missouri, Mother Nature reclaimed the land it lost to man and recovered it in an amazingly short amount of time.

Any travel was slow going. There weren't many paths, just an occasional game trail. He followed a meandering stream, stomach growling ominously, hoping for a shot at a Whitetail deer. As he rounded a large oak tree, whose trunk was nearly five feet across, he glimpsed a pool of water ahead. The pool was beautiful, surrounded by high cattails, vines, and forest fern, with water chuckling in from an outcropping of lichen-covered limestone on the high side.

It was a beautiful scene of a natural green grotto in the forest—but not nearly as beautiful as the girl kneeling in the clear water. The pool was in a small lime-stone basin and almost completely hidden from all directions. If he'd come to it from any other way, he might have missed her.

He watched, mesmerized, as the girl washed herself with a mat of moss and then submerged to rinse off, coming up to catch the few rays of sunlight in her spun gold hair, water running rivulets down her tawny body. High breasted and slim-hipped, this vision contrasted sharply with the camp followers in raider camps he was used to seeing, or even women in the few settlements that were springing up. He suddenly realized the girl in the pool was Katherine.

He stood for uncounted minutes, unabashedly watching the girl in the pool. All the old memories—the wants and desires, hearth and home, children playing, the sharing—all the things he ever dreamed of came bursting through his veins in a flash of emotion. For a moment, his senses reeled just from the sheer desire of something so normal again.

Silently easing through the underbrush, he found her pile of clothing. With a small smile, he made some adjustments.

While he watched her, she'd turned her back to him. Now she turned again and stood to come out of the pool. Her hands were up in her hair, twisting it into a braid and squeezing the water out. The blond hair, darkened by the water, was long, with a natural healthy sheen few women had anymore. She looked around the perimeter of the pool, testing the breeze like an animal.

The one place she didn't look was toward him, which gave him the only clue of what came next.

Suddenly, as she got closer, she lunged in a flat dive

for her weapons. Her hands hit the pile of clothes, and she came up with the Browning semi-automatic in one hand and her knife in the other. Facing Trent, who was sitting nonchalantly on a rock, she bore no resemblance to the silky Lilith who had just been bathing in the pool. With eyes hard as agate, she stood in a fighter's stance. Her hair clung wetly to her neck and fell across her chest, but didn't conceal the dirt and leaves sticking to her breasts and upper part of her body. Her eyes were wide with adrenaline—blue ice on white snow.

Her breathing started to settle down as she recognized him and decided he didn't present any immediate danger. The smile he was giving her, and the appreciative gaze over her body, didn't do anything to improve her disposition.

"Enjoying the show?" Her voice was soft and throaty.

He chuckled. "Oh, yes."

She thumbed back the hammer on the Browning. "Get out of here."

"Not yet." Trent smiled a little larger.

She pulled the trigger, and the hammer fell on an empty chamber. There was no change in her expression, the usual widening of the eyes just before action, no warning at all. Just...click.

The second surprise came when, without any hesitation, she threw the empty pistol at him and then followed it in with her knife, cutting edge up. Anyone watching would have laughed as he awkwardly lunged backward off the rock. The first sweep with her knife threatened decapitation, and then she came right over the rock and landed in the middle of him while he was still rolling. They came to a stop with her on top, knife ready to plunge, but the barrel of his pistol nestled under her chin.

"Mine is loaded," he said, trying to catch his breath after she landed on his chest.

Water dripped from her hair onto his face as she panted in anger as much as the exertion. Her breath smelled of the spearmint leaves she had been chewing earlier in the day, and her eyes were level, shining hard with resolve. For a minute, he thought she'd try it. She was mad and scared, and it was in her to try to end it right here, and decide her fate with her own hand.

Gradually, a little sanity returned, and her eyes turned wary because she had seen something in his eyes, too. He would kill her, and she was not ready to die.

"Easy, Katherine. Let's not make any mistakes."

With her weight settled in on top of him and her breasts swinging above his face, he was having a real hard time keeping his mind on the matter at hand. Slowly, keeping the gun at her throat, he rolled her off onto her side and took her knife. Nearly identical to his, it would have gutted him easily. As he knelt over her, seeing the fear and dread start in her eyes, he suddenly realized what she expected next.

Standing up, he reached down and took her arm, pulling her to her feet. He looked straight into her eyes. She didn't shrink away from him or try to cover herself. She stood defiant before him, and he liked her even more for it.

He thought how his attempt at a little fun almost turned disastrous. "Look." He smiled at her. "I am sorry. I was out of line, and it was a poor joke. But you should know better than this...whatever you are thinking. I'm not going to hurt you."

"Why should I know better?" she said hotly, her angry gestures making her jiggle in places he tried not to watch. "I don't even know you."

"You will," he said gruffly and gave her a gentle shove back toward the water. "Wash up and get dressed."

She looked at him, still doubting, speculation furrowing her brow.

"We'll talk when you're dressed."

As she looked at him wonderingly, he walked away. She suddenly realized she was standing naked and rushed back to the pool and her clothes.

A short distance away, he saw a shallow depression where an old cedar grew up against a bluff and would diffuse the small amount of smoke from the hatful of fire he built. He went to retrieve his pack and put some water on to boil. The place he chose was concealed from a casual observer and was the best he could do at the time.

Looking up, he saw the girl standing by the fire. Shifting her weight from one foot to the other, she looked like she might bolt away at any moment. He noticed she had her weapons, though.

"You took my bullets." Her tone indicated he would also suck eggs and eat skunks.

Trent reached into his pouch and brought out the magazine of .380s. Handing her the shells, he smiled slightly and said, "Sorry."

"Sure you are," she said sarcastically.

"You should have known, you know, by the weight. You need to learn that. And the spring is weak in the clip. It'll misfire one day."

He went quietly about making a stew. He had bagged a rabbit earlier, so he put that in the wooden pot, along with arrow weed bulbs and wild onions.

"You followed me, didn't you?"

"Yes, I did." She stared at him until he shrugged. "I thought to make sure you got to base camp alright." Then he smiled. "I didn't expect to find you in the pool. Lost my head, I guess."

"Is that all you were doing? Nothing else on your mind?"

"Of course not." His eyes met hers. "I admit it. I want to know you. Satisfied? I was afraid I wouldn't see you again, and for some reason, that bothered me."

"You said I should know you wouldn't hurt me. How, Trent? Like I said, I don't know you. All I know is what I have heard, and that's not been too good." She hesitated a moment, then sighed noisily. "Alright. I'm a big girl. I won't deny I'm attracted to you. Sort of. But the things I hear...I'm not sure I *want* to know you."

"I understand." He nodded. *Attracted to him?* "You are entirely correct, and I'm sorry."

"And you shouldn't sneak up on people." He could see a ghost of a smile forming—just a twitch at the corner of her lips.

He grinned at her. "Somehow, I think you're going to make me do irrational things."

After studying him a minute, she sat cross-legged across the fire from him and studied the pot of boiling water. "Why doesn't the wood burn?"

"Won't, as long as the fire stays below the water line. The water absorbs the heat."

"Why not use a metal pot? There are plenty of old camping supplies around."

"It's too dangerous. Metal shines and rattles in your pack when you bump it, so I don't carry it."

She looked at him in wonderment. "Are you always so careful?"

"Hope to be...likely die if I'm not."

The girl sat across the fire from him, slowly relaxing, and leaned forward to smell the stew. "Whatever is in there, it smells pretty good." She looked at him. "I can do better."

"No doubt." He glanced at her seriously. "Pretty sure of yourself, aren't you?"

Her chin came up defiantly. "I've survived so far."

He looked at her levelly. "Through no fault of your own. What if I'd been someone else? Anyone could have followed you, and then you would be dead or something worse. And lady, you saw what something worse could be like, back down the trail."

She tried to hold his eyes but failed. "Why didn't you?"

"What?"

Her head snapped up. "Rape me. Kill me. Take your pick."

"Not my style." He gave her another quick grin. "If we ever get together, I want you to enjoy it."

She abruptly gave him a radiant smile as he looked warily at her. "Well, I'm glad you didn't. Thank you." She fidgeted around and suddenly seemed to have nowhere to go with her hands. "You're sure getting your eyes full. You acted the same back at the clearing where we found Markie. Haven't you seen a woman in a while?"

He snapped out of his stare. "No, actually, I haven't. At least, not a woman as beautiful as you."

She settled back against a rock with a pensive look. "So, John Trent, what do we do now?"

"We rest. We talk. Then, we see." He grinned at her. "Who knows, you might get to like me."

———

AS SHE SAT, cradling a cup of coffee in her hands, made from the one metal utensil in his pack—a coffee pot so blackened by campfires it had ceased to shine, she marveled at how peaceful the forest seemed. She was surprised at herself for being able to relax with a stranger, alone in the forest. Although she admitted to herself, he did not seem like a stranger. It had been a long time since she had any coffee to drink, other than the brew made from chicory root, and for this moment at least, she was determined to enjoy it.

The quietness of the forest settled in. First light, and evening, was always this way. The mist hung over the ground, swirling slightly in the breeze. Birds called, and the smells of the forest were always the strongest at the beginning, or end, of the day.

She shook leaves from her hair, and on impulse, let out the braids she had hurriedly put together. Taking a comb from her pack, she ran it through her hair, looking speculatively at Trent. In a rugged way, he was handsome, although older than her. His age did not matter to her, but it sure would with her father. She caught him looking at her again and felt a sudden pull toward those gray eyes and quick hands. "It's quiet here."

"Yes, it seems that way. But the forest is alive with sound. You just have to learn to notice it. In the old days, there was so much noise around you couldn't hear anything, and silence actually scared people. They called it noise pollution. Not a problem anymore."

She thought for a moment, watching the man in front of her. He appeared relaxed and like a coiled spring at the same time. Curious. "You sound almost glad things have changed."

"I can like the changes without liking the way it came about."

She watched him clean his guns. "Why do you give so much attention to your guns? Why keep them so clean? Twice I have seen you, and both times you worked on your guns."

"This new world we've got, sometimes these guns are the only thing between me and being dead. I don't want to be dead." He looked at her pensively. "Especially now."

In the silence that followed, she smiled at him, knowing she was making him uncomfortable. Perversely, she wondered if he had a woman and if she made him uncomfortable, too. She surprised herself by a quick feeling of jealousy. *Why should she care?*

"I should move soon." His statement was belied when he didn't move at all. Maybe he thought sitting with her made the trail not so inviting.

She could see him come to a decision. "I'm going to find a place to sleep for the night. You're welcome to come along if you want. Your choice."

"What's wrong with this spot?"

He just shrugged at her. "We've been here too long, and it's too exposed."

She looked at him speculatively, knowing she should be leaving, but now the circumstances changed. Now, she was the one reluctant to leave. Something important was happening here. "I'll tag along. For a while, anyway."

———

THEY MOVED out with Trent in the lead. Disdaining the game trails, he weaved a path through the thick undergrowth, constantly keeping an eye out for a place to spend the night. They would have a cold camp, with no fire to attract attention. Discomfort was another price of survival. Cooking was done during the day, then camp was moved somewhere else to lessen the chance of discovery. These days, you never wanted anyone to see you before you saw them.

As they rode, he was impressed with the girl behind him. She hadn't said a word since they left, keeping quiet on the trail. He could smell her, though, and knew what she looked like without seeing her. He could *feel* her. For once in his life, he didn't know how to proceed. All he knew was he wanted this girl.

They found a spot under a white oak. The canopy of leaves would keep the dampness off, and the wide expanse of dried leaves on the ground would give warning if anything approached.

It wasn't only people they had to worry about. This was a land of black bear, wild pigs, and more than once he'd seen the tawny mountain lion, any of which would be hard to handle, especially at night.

He cleared away a couple of places of leaves and sticks, making sure no rocks were sticking up. After staking out the horses, he wordlessly wrapped himself in his blanket and taking a last look around, was immediately asleep.

————

KATIE SAT for a while staring at the man. He slept lightly. Every time she'd make a slight rustling noise, his breathing would pause and then resume. She looked around her, wishing she had another cup of coffee, but settled for a drink from her canteen.

Reviewing the events of the day, she shook her head slowly in the darkness and smiled. A woman needs a man just as much as he needs her. Unless she missed her guess, this was quite a man. Maybe, just maybe...

———

DUST ROSE in lazy clouds from their horse's hooves as four men pulled their mounts up in front of the rundown shack centered in the clearing. Slouched in their saddles, the men surveyed the area, looking for signs of life in the adjoining buildings. The barn was falling in and the attached stock pens were overgrown with weeds. The forest was slowly winning the battle to take back the clearing. Smoke rose slowly from the chimney of the house.

"You better be right about this one, Pagan." Red Seaver's voice took on a plaintive note. "The woman at the last place we hit was downright ugly, and fattern' a cow."

The other men snickered until Pagan Reeves silenced them with a glance. "I didn't know you were so particular, Red."

"He ain't," one of the other men spoke loudly, grinning and spitting a wad of tobacco into the weeds.

"Hello, the house." Pagan's voice echoed in the small clearing. When no response came, he said conversationally, "I know you're in there, McCracken. You don't come out, well just burn this shack down around your ears."

The front door slowly creaked open, and a gaunt man

dressed in bib overalls stepped onto the porch. A floppy hat came down to his ears, and his bare feet were stark white against the weathered boards of the porch. He held a shotgun in one hand pointed at the floor. "I told you last time, Pagan. We want no part of you." The man's voice dripped with Arkansas drawl.

Pagan grinned at him. "Don't matter a bit, McCracken. You had your chance. That's gone now. So, why don't you call out your women? Me and the boys would like to get acquainted."

"What do you...?" The man stopped short at the sight of Pagan's gun on him. Casually, grinning widely, the other men drew their weapons.

"Drop the shotgun."

Nervously, the settler started sidling toward the door until a shot from Pagan's gun splintered the boards in front of him. The shotgun fell to the floor next to his bloodied feet.

Immediately, Red and the others jumped from their mounts and swarmed onto the porch. One of the men knocked McCracken senseless with the butt of a pistol as they brushed past him into the house.

Moments later, they emerged, towing two kicking and screaming women behind them.

"Now this is more like it." Red was holding the younger of the two girls. His hands pulled up her blouse, roughly squeezing and fondling her. Both girls were crying, looking at their father lying next to the house.

Pagan dismounted and walked up to the girls. Stopping at the older girl, he reached out and gently cupped one of her breasts. He spoke without turning his head. "Big, you and Smith keep watch for a while. Red and I have the first call on these ladies."

Big Waters started to grumble, but a glance from Pagan shut him up. "You'll get your turn as many times as you want."

As the youngest girl started to scream, Red silenced her with a slap.

"Hey," Waters shouted at him as they rode to the outskirts of the clearing. "Don't mess them up too much."

———

THE SUN WAS SLIDING past noon, leaving scant shadows around Pagan as he sat on a stump out in the yard. The girls were cleaning up after the meager meal they'd been forced to prepare for the men. Both were naked, and the younger girl had blood running down one leg.

Standing, Pagan motioned to the men. "We better be going. We're burning daylight, boys." He looked at Red. "You know what to do with them, don't you, Red?"

Red grinned as he pulled his knife. "Oh, I surely do."

"No. Don't hurt them anymore, Pagan." The muffled and anguished cry came from the bound father.

"You should have joined us when you had the chance, McCracken."

"You people are vermin. Not fit to live on this earth. Someday you will get yours. I just wish I'd be there to see it." The man's voice choked with emotion and his own blood. "Girls? I am sorry, girls. I should've done better for you." He strained to see his daughters, who were huddled in a corner.

"Red, do the girls first, so McCracken can watch," Pagan said.

HOURS LATER, the four men reined in their lathered horses at a junction in the trail.

"We'll split up here. Red, you take the men and head for Big Springs. Look around for some more people to recruit. You know the kind we want." Pagan's tone was terse, his mind on other things.

"Where you goin'?"

"I think it's time to pay another visit to the Sanchez ranch." He grinned at them.

The men exchanged grins. "I know what you're after. That Sanchez woman is mighty fine looking."

"Forget it, boys. That's one I won't share. Besides, if we get all her cattle, we'll have all the women we want." He stopped at the edge of the forest. "Red, you see Hobbs, you send him to base camp after that bartender—what's his name, Walsh? He's been giving Colonel what's-his-name too much information. Time we put a stop to it."

Red raised his hand in answer and jogged his horse down the trail with Big Waters and Jumbo Smith.

FOUR

TRENT RODE into the east side of Base Camp Bravo, leaving the protection of the forest and the things he understood—half sliding his horse down the rocky embankment and scattering leaves onto Farm Road AP. He let his horse blow a moment as he reacquainted himself with the layout of the Army base Colonel Bonham put together a few years ago.

Shunning the main roads, the Colonel had put his camp right in the middle of the part of Mark Twain National Forest skirting the White Fork River. Equal distance between Vanzant to the west and Burnham to the east, the camp was just a wide place in the road, containing a few buildings and storage bunkers. All this, surrounded by the rolling hills and forest of the Ozark Mountains. The Colonel had chosen this location for its remoteness and easy accessibility to the forest he hoped to control.

As a primary mission, Base Camp Bravo was to make seasoned soldiers out of raw recruits sent from the plague-ravished land back east, and, somehow, by their very presence, bring law and order to the new frontier.

Base Camp Bravo was reachable by vehicle if you had gas, which most did not. The Army had meager supplies of fuel, hoarded and confiscated from civilians, but those supplies were for very special occasions.

This must be one of those occasions, Trent thought. He watched slightly amazed, while a green truck, the back covered with a green tarpaulin, disgorged a squad of men dressed in green clothes, faces streaked with dark green paint, and carrying mottled green packs on their backs full of the standard Army issue of useless equipment. It had been a long time since the jungles of Central America. The lessons learned, and paid for by blood, still ignored.

He rode toward the main building where he hoped to give his dispatches to Colonel Bonham, passing by the soldiers on the way. He carefully looked them over as he rode by. All had packs piled high on their backs. With the packs catching on every tree limb they passed, coupled with wearing a steel pot on their heads, those men would be deaf and blind in the forest while their enemies would be able to hear them coming hundreds of yards away. Trent saw one man looking at his SATCOM navigation gear, while another was calibrating motion and heat sensors. Amazing. Useless.

The variety of expression was typical. Some looked at him with scorn, some with suspicion, most with open hostility. He knew the drill. He'd been part of it once, so he could walk the walk and talk the talk. He wasn't dressed like them. Therefore, he wasn't with them. Anyone not with them was against them. Their confidence in themselves revealed a subtle arrogance, the result of superior weapons and training...they thought. What they didn't know was how inadequate their training was. Fire teams and massive firepower would not save them in the dense forest. They would need to think to adapt. And fight. Fight as they'd never dreamed. Hopefully, they would learn. If they lived.

Guiding his horse from shade to shade, tree to tree, he finally ended his roundabout route under the spreading arms of a box elder tree. He tied the reins to a branch and threw the saddlebags across his shoulders. Finding his way into the building, he walked down a short corridor. The floor shined enough that he could see his face in it. Some things never change. There was a desk at the end of the hall, manned by a starched young private busily trying to look important as Trent approached.

"Colonel in?"

The man looked at him, wrinkling his nose a little at the smell. You don't ride a sweaty horse all day without picking up a little fragrance along the way.

"Not here." Nonchalant. He didn't care.

Trent stared at him until the young man started to show color in his cheeks from the inspection.

"Son, suppose you got a place for these dispatches? The Colonel will want to see them."

Jumping to his feet, the private took the bags, a slow warming of respect in his eyes. Even new recruits knew about couriers. "You could have told me you were a courier. I thought you were one of the locals, in to beg food or ammo from the Colonel."

"Not likely." He turned away, adding over his shoulder. "I'll be at the Bucket if he wants me."

He took his horse to the white-boarded corral and turned it loose. Carrying his saddle and extra pack into the barn, he was accosted by a shriveled imp of a man wearing faded overalls and sporting a long tobacco-stained white beard. Trent idly wondered how long it would be before the old and battered gimme' cap, with the picture of a green tractor on it, would move.

"Thought you was dead, Trent. All them raiders must be gettin' soft, lettin' you traipse around the country all the time." He moved his green baseball cap to sit jauntily on the back of his head. *About ten seconds.*

He gave the old man a wry grin. "Got close a couple of times. How've you been, Pop?"

"Been better—been worse." The old man cackled, showing stained teeth, and pulled the cap level again.

"All right to leave my stuff here?" He had no idea when he was moving out again, but knew all his gear would be safe with the old man. "Maybe overnight?"

"Just a night? You go over to the Bucket, you may not come back for a week. I hear they's a new batch of girls over there." He smiled wickedly, shifting his cap around. "Wouldn't know myself, of course. Too old, you know?"

Trent grinned at him, shaking his head in mock amazement. Tossing his pack in a corner, he pulled the magazine from his AK and locked back the bolt, ejecting the round from the barrel. Catching the spinning cartridge in the air, he replaced it in the magazine and dropped the rifle on top of the pile.

"You still got that old gun? Why ain't you got one of the new fancy Colt guns the Army's givin' away, or one of them AK-90s you can find layin' about? There's something called the M-4 that's really sweet, too. I think I've seen every kind of rifle in the world go through here."

"How many still work with dirty and old ammo?" He looked at his rifle with affection. The old assault rifle, with its folding stock and snap under bayonet, had seen a lot of use. Even so, it was still accurate to a thousand yards and a formidable weapon. Of more importance, it used the most common ammunition found in the United States or the world: the 7.62mm NATO round. "These old 47s, you can pick one up out of a mud hole and it still works. This one hasn't worn out yet. I put bullets in it, and the thing goes 'boom' when I want it to."

"Know what you mean, I guess. Though, I never could figure it. Army boys take a gun that's supposed to be accurate to halfway roun' the world, shoots from now to next week, then they duck into the woods with it where you can't see more'n fifteen feet, an' if you can't get it done with one shot...hell, you won't get another. Don't make sense."

The old man's eyes clouded over as his mind went down memory lane. The cap shifted to a more serious angle.

"I remember how it was in the nineties. Street price on that gun was sixty bucks, with a box of five hundred rounds of ammo for another twenty. There must have been thousands of them. Had a sign over in the hardware store—war surplus AKs and SKS rifles...only dropped once."

Chuckling at his own humor, the old man moved his cap to the back of his head and waddled back into the barn, his skinny legs bowed like parentheses.

As Trent was leaving, he turned and asked the old man, "Seen a young girl come in? Tall, blond, well set up, and riding a mouse-colored gelding?"

The old man shook his head. "Nope. Wished I had. I get lonely at night."

"Yeah, keep wishing." He laughed as he passed

through the door. The day before, Katie had decided to go on ahead of him to base camp. She said she needed to think. Whatever that meant.

"Won't do no good to watch for her. If she sees me first, she'll never look at you again." Sharp eyes contemplated him a moment. "Hey," the old man shouted at Trent's retreating back. "You ain't getting soft on some woodsy girl, are you?"

He could hear the old man cackling for a block.

———

THE BUCKET-O-BLOOD HAD SPRUNG UP OVERNIGHT, EVEN faster than the base camp. Running pack trains into the deserted cities, Charley Walsh brought fresh supplies of liquor and hard goods into the camp almost weekly. His place was always crowded, the noise level maintained a dull roar, and today proved no exception. He had two things making the frontier bearable for men who didn't really want to be there, women and liquor.

Trent paused at the doorway, wiping sweat from his forehead as his eyes adjusted to the dim lighting in the room. Settling his webbed duty belt, he stopped long enough to tie the leather thong, at the bottom of his holster, around his thigh. He kept the thong untied while riding, mostly out of convenience. Now, it might make all the difference if he needed his gun in a hurry. He had Velcro fasteners once. They were easy to use, but once dirt got in them...modern and new wasn't always better.

Most of the tables were full, but there was not much of a crowd at the front bar. He planted his elbows on the countertop, hooked his heel on the foot rail, and yelled at the bald-headed man at the end of the bar. "Can a man get a drink around here?"

Charley turned around with a smile. "Trent." He said the word like it was a puzzle and he had all the answers. "You made it back."

"Some reason you thought I wouldn't?"

The two men shook hands, a slow grasp of friends who had not seen each other for a while.

"Did you bring good news or bad?"

"Little of both," Trent said with aplomb. "The good news is the forest is still there, green and beautiful as ever, cool and quiet. You should see the deer. They are multiplying like rabbits. The game is coming back, Charley. A man couldn't starve out there if he tried."

"Okay, so what's the bad news?"

"The bad news is—the raiders still own it."

"Yeah, I hear you." He had always dreamed of living in a cabin, high on a mountain so he could just sit and watch the world go to hell.

"So, what's going on in base camp, Charley?"

"You didn't notice?" Charley's voice sounded disgusted. "Didn't you see all the Mr. *Green Jeans* traipsing around like they owned the place? They just keep pouring in but don't go anywhere."

Mr. Green Jeans was the name the natives had given the US Army's finest. Green being the uniform of the day, of course.

"Any news from back east?" He was like everyone else —always wanting news of how things were back in "the world."

"Same as usual, from what I hear. Industry is picking up a little, and most of the plague is gone. Although I've been hearing rumbles from some of the new recruits that particular nightmare is coming back. Thank God, the bacterial rot never came back. Things are so peaceful back in the real world, the Army has run out of things to do. They are going to launch a campaign out here to save us all from ourselves. Now you know why so many extra troops are around. They just can't understand how we can live without them."

"Who's going to save the Army?" The two men laughed together. They'd discussed this subject before.

Walsh jutted his chin at the recruits surrounding one of the tables. "Not this bunch."

He chuckled and said, "I saw Pops over at the livery. How old is he, Charley?"

"Dunno. Looks an even hundred, but he is probably not a day over ninety-nine. They say he's been through it all."

"Looks to me like someone soaked him until he shrunk. I have never seen so many wrinkles on one human in my life."

Charley's expression clouded over. "Trent, you ever wonder how it would have been if the plague didn't hit the world so hard? I mean, if things had gone on the same as before? I found an old newspaper the other day. Reading about it was downright depressing. Seems like everything quit working at once, and people just couldn't believe what was happening; runaway virus that medicine couldn't stop, super strains of bacteria dissolving flesh, for Christ's sake. Sometimes I..."

"Charley..."

The man looked at him, startled out of his reverie.

"Just let it go, partner." He knew what the man was feeling, had felt it himself too many times to count. "You can't change it. We have to take the world the way it is, not the way it was. Just let it go."

"Yeah." Charley slowly perked up. "Hell, yes. I almost lost it for a minute. It just doesn't do any good to think about it."

He'd been looking over the people in the room while conversing with Walsh. Thinking of the murdered girl, he looked at the people around him with new eyes. Eyes that were, at the same time, jaded and curious. Who could do such a thing? What would they be like? How would they act in public? Jumbled thoughts bounced around in his head as he scanned the small crowd.

For the most part, the clientele wasn't any different from those found in other various settlements around the interior. Nearly everyone in the large room wore a uniform of some sort, and carrying weapons were second nature to them. The exceptions were the working girls. They weren't wearing much of anything, and he couldn't see how they could possibly hide a weapon. *Thinking of which.* "Charley, you see a tall blond come into town in the last day or so? Good looking, maybe six feet tall, looking to buy supplies?"

"That's a big girl." Charley thought a moment, his face screwed up in the palm of his hand. "Nope. 'Course, the only women coming in here are usually looking for a job. Are we talking about that kind of girl?"

"Not likely. At least, I don't think so." His mind was already back in the crowd and his answer preoccupied, as his attention was drawn to a table occupied by a group of yelling, screaming recruits out to set a new record for good times. At a table next to them were four hard-eyed men conspicuous by what they were *not* doing. Trent pointed with his chin at the somber group. "What's the story on them?"

Charley cast a worried glance their way, then leaned closer to Trent. "Best leave them alone. They ain't locals, and they sure as hell ain't Army. All I know is they came in here about an hour ago, parked at a table, and didn't even order a drink."

Looking at the men, he thought they were more likely wolves in sheep's clothing, or raiders doing a little scouting of their own. He wondered suddenly just how many soldiers were in camp. It would be embarrassing to have the soldiers out looking for raiders while the raiders took the camp. He decided that would be a good question for the Colonel.

The door to the saloon pushed open, and a man stepped through that put Trent on full alert. Looking around the gloomy interior of the room, the man went directly to the table they were worried about and sat down. He knew what they were, now. Mercs. And Ben Hobbs would be the worst of them.

New interest held him now, and he quietly slid his drink away. While acting as if he was rubbing a sore leg, he casually slipped the thong off the hammer of his pistol. The leather thong kept the gun from falling out of the holster accidentally, but if he needed the gun in a hurry, there wouldn't be time to take it off. He was a careful man—he'd helped bury men who weren't.

Hobbs was a mercenary for hire. Sometimes he worked for settlers, occasionally he ran with raiders, but usually he worked for himself. He was bad all the time, and couldn't be trusted. Although he hadn't heard much about him lately, he knew any place Ben Hobbs would be, there was going to be trouble.

———

WALSH SAW Trent move his drink away. His eyes narrowed as he felt a subtle change come over the room, prompting him to move casually toward his shotgun, kept under the bar. A couple of men who lived in the high-up hills with their families got up, nodded to him, and walked unhurriedly through the back door—other men squared around so they could watch the front. The party of recruits were blissfully unaware of anything going on around them. Charley felt his mouth go dry. He knew something was going to happen, it was just a matter of when.

Amid a peal of laughter, one of the soldiers suddenly scooted back his chair and jostled one of the mercs at the other table. Slowly the man stood up, his spilled drink making a dark splotch on his pants and shirt. He had a semi-auto handgun strapped to his waist and held a folded-up Mac-10 machine pistol in his hands. "You sojer boys are cutting it kind of wide, ain't you?"

The young soldier looked stupidly at him, his mouth working like a fish out of water as he tried to think of something to say. He was too drunk to hear the danger signals going off in his head, or see the situation he was in.

Finally, he just laughed. "What?"

"I said you are a piece of shit." The merc was just waiting as if he had already choreographed the scene.

The young soldier let out a growl and slammed up from his chair as the rest of the men at his table stood up, watching the byplay. None were armed.

As the soldier came up, the merc slashed him across

the face with the MAC-10, showering the table with blood.

"Hold it." Charley held his shotgun across his chest, the barrel pointed at the ceiling. "You just hold it." His voice was loud in the suddenly quiet room. "There will be no fighting in here. Understood?"

———

TRENT, watching carefully, suddenly realized Charley was out of position. From the position he held the shotgun, he wouldn't be able to get it into action fast enough.

With an unholy glint in his eyes, the merc was bringing the machine pistol up.

If he cuts loose in these close quarters... Trent moved into action.

Nothing in the world is louder than the sound of a gun cocking from an unexpected direction. The sound of the hammer rocking back on his pistol froze the merc. His eyes were steady on Charley, but he dearly needed to look back at Trent. He was caught in his own trap, and afraid to move. Turning his head slightly, the merc could see him out of the corner of his eyes, noticed the light glinting off the pistol, and saw the dark bore of the barrel pointing straight at him. The hole seemed to be getting bigger every second, and the merc began to sweat.

"Ben Hobbs." Trent hesitated a moment as the name echoed in the room, then said conversationally, "Call him off."

He was looking directly at the mercs. All the men were waiting for something to happen, holding weapons in their laps instead of holsters. It looked like a setup, and he suddenly realized the target was Charley, but he wasn't sure why. It really didn't matter. Charley was game enough, but he was not a fighter. And Charley Walsh was his friend.

Finally, Hobbs said, "Forget it."

The merc slowly straightened, the barrel of the MAC-10 jerking toward the ceiling. His tawny eyes found Trent in the gloomy room. "Some other time?"

"No." He didn't intend to be suckered into a needless fight.

"How about now, outside?"

"Mister." His voice was cold. "I don't even know you. Why be in such a hurry to die?"

The man's eyes were wild, and he had a sudden thought about drugs, which was one of two things you didn't see much of anymore. The second thing was fat people.

"Well, I cain't dance." The merc grinned at him—taunting him. "The stock market's all busted. Mr. Green Jeans done stole all the gas for my four-wheeler, and I ain't killed a man in a week. I guess I just need the entertainment."

"Forget it." He turned and resumed his position at the bar, never losing sight of the merc in the mirror.

The man stood uncertainly for a moment before sitting down, banging his MAC-10 on the table. As the gun bounced and clattered, the men around the table flinched. Hobbs quickly reached out and set the safety on.

Hobbs and his men conversed in a low murmur, and then they all got up together and strode from the room. Collective sighs of relief went around from the rest of the patrons.

He walked over to the table of recruits. All of them were now stone-cold sober.

"You wanna-be soldiers, listen to me." His voice was level and cold. "Don't you *ever*..." He paused to let his words sink in. "*Ever* go anywhere without your weapon. Your weapon is the first thing you pick up in the morning and the last thing you lay down at night. You sleep with it like it's the best lover you ever had."

He suddenly yelled at them. "Do you understand?"

The recruits flinched back in their chairs, and he turned back toward the bar amid a chorus of yessir's from the table.

"I thought we was going to have to shoot that boy." Walsh's voice was matter of fact.

"So did I. Charley, have you made anyone mad lately? This was a setup if ever I saw one. They wanted you."

"Don't know." Charley scratched his head quizzically. "Been helping the Colonel some. Lettin' him know who was on the up and up around here, that sort of thing. Nothin' serious."

"Someone must have taken it seriously."

Again, the door banged open, but this time it was the young private from the Colonel's office. He strode purposefully into the room. *Definitely a man on a mission.*

"Colonel's compliments, Mr. Trent. He'd like to see you in his office."

Charley snorted into the beer he'd just poured for himself. "Ain't he purty, John? Don't you just feel safe all over with him running about?"

He tossed his drink off, gave Charley a grin, and strode out the door, with the private right on his heels— and walked right into trouble.

The merc from the bar was standing in the middle of the street, legs spread, hands brushing the butt of his pistol. Maybe he saw one of those old western vids and loved the look of it. Maybe he was just crazy. Trent sighed softly. This was nuts. It wasn't over.

The hard voice of the merc rang between the buildings. "I heard you was something with a gun, woods runner. I'd like to see just how good."

He looked at him calmly. After the first rush of adrenaline, his nerves always steadied out. His heart was beating a slow sixty. He had been down this road before.

"You don't want to do this, son."

"Really?" The merc was shouting, grandstanding to his audience. "I can take you any day."

"Then, do it," Trent said simply. He never saw any sense in talking when it was time to fight.

The merc had probably found an unbroken mirror somewhere. He cut quite a picture with his low-slung gun in a tactical web-holster and fast draw. He dreamed of being famous, of fear and respect from people on the frontier. But he never dreamed of the years of hard work or the kind of fire it takes to mold and temper a truly dangerous man. And he never dreamed of dying. He just couldn't picture himself dead in that mirror.

As the merc's hand stabbed for the autoloader holstered at his side, Trent seemed to react in slow motion, at least he knew it would appear that way. Time walked with measured cadence for the people who watched along the street. Even as his gun was sweeping up, he checked to make sure bystanders were out of the line of fire. He then stepped to the right to clear himself from the young soldier who had unwittingly bumped into him from behind. Most of the people watching thought he had waited too long.

A single shot echoed up and down the street. He heard one of the bar girls gasp, hand to her mouth as she looked at him, probably sure he was dead. But there wasn't any blood on him, and he was holding his gun steady on the merc.

The merc slowly bent at the middle, a macabre bow at the end of a poor performance. He hadn't even got a shot off. The merc raised his eyes to look at him, and then crumpled face down in the street. Tail up, and nose in the dirt, he was dead.

He shifted his gun to cover the group across the street. He and Hobbs locked eyes across the narrow street. Hobbs's right hand was on his half-drawn gun, and his men were waiting, their eagerness to kill apparent in their faces. "Any reason I shouldn't kill you, too, Hobbs? You put that boy up to this." His voice was hard.

When Hobbs spoke, his voice was a painful rasp. "I'd just as soon not die today, Trent."

"Then take your hand away from the gun."

Hobbs's hand moved as if jerked by a rope. His pistol fell back into its nylon holster. Trent's single-action was still lined on his belly.

He abruptly chuckled. "Reckon you owe me one, Hobbs."

The man stared angrily at him a moment, then turned and walked away. His men followed more slowly, casting murderous looks between their fallen comrade and Trent.

He was surprised. They'd lost face twice in the last hour. Any self-respecting group of bad boys could not afford that. People might get the wrong idea and think they were soft.

Holstering his gun, Trent walked toward the Colonel's office. The private didn't follow him so closely this time. As they passed the livery doorway, he called inside. "Pops, put that rifle away. I like to shot you when that barrel poked out the window."

Pops's shrill cackle echoed from deep within the barn. He wondered if the cap was back or forward. Probably forward. Maybe.

FIVE

THE OLD BUILDING shuddered from the storm within its walls. The office seemed to expand, forcing dust from the nooks and crannies of ill-fitting lumber by the sheer force of noise. Army personnel standing guard at different points in the building avoided looking at each other and turtled their heads down a little tighter to their shoulders. Lieutenant Saints, who just sat down outside the door, got up and walked up the hall away from the noise.

Along the hall were wooden chairs available for people waiting to see the Colonel. The girl sitting in one of the chairs shook her head at the adjutant's invitation to go with him. She sat smiling, hands folded across her stomach, legs stretched out and crossed at the ankles, listening to the tirade going on inside.

The Army colonel behind the desk in the exploding office was getting older by the minute, his face swollen in rage, blood pressure at record levels for a man still alive and standing.

"Christ on a pogo stick, Trent! Have you gone insane? You going raider on me? Losing your grip? What in God's name are you trying to do? Kill all the raiders by yourself? Are you crazy? I watched that little scene out the window. What was that? Code Duello? Shootout at the OK Corral? Jesus, Trent."

The words launched at the man lounging in the solitary chair in front of the desk were delivered with enough force to make a private in a foreign army thousands of miles away snap to attention.

Trent could not keep the smile off his face as he contemplated the irreverent picture conjured up by the Army colonel. Leave it to an ex-drill instructor to come up with something like that. The smile did not quite extend to his eyes. Eyes were a picture into the soul and that was a haunted land with too many memories, and too much death.

"Conversation kind of dried up, Frank." His was voice soft, in contrast to the verbal fusillade coming from his superior, echoing through the building like a thunderstorm over the horizon. Too many had made the mistake of thinking he was like his voice. Too many had died trying to figure out the difference.

———

FRANK BONHAM, a field colonel retired to a desk job by a host of 7.62mm pieces of lead fired from an AK-47, glared at the man lounging in the chair before him. John knew what he saw. An enigma. A throwback. Born two centuries too late.

The Colonel finally wore down, bringing his

breathing back to normal, glaring intensely at him. The man before him always rankled his sense of honor and fair play, even when he'd been married to his daughter. But he was so damned good at what he did. His gun, an old single-action revolver if you can believe it, was so damned fast. What had he read in an old novel? The sibilant whisper of snake-fast hands? Most men carried some brand of autoloader. Fourteen or nineteen shots as fast as they could pull the trigger. Trent told him you just need one shot. If you need more than that, it's time to 'beat feet and get out of Dodge.'

He didn't often play by the rules, albeit rules being freshly made up or rekindled from the old days. Usually, they just didn't seem to apply. His honor was a closely-knit thing that only Trent could fathom, and he didn't share much.

He watched him unwind his lanky frame from the wooden chair, finally standing in front of the desk, making a visible effort at straightening sore muscles and stiff joints.

"Trent, you can't just up and shoot people like that," the Colonel said, his voice and blood pressure finally within reasonable limits.

"What would you like me to do, Frank? He was a hard case, a merc for hire, and Ben Hobbs was out there with him. I don't know what his problem was, maybe he just didn't like the way I put on my hat. It doesn't matter because I didn't have any choice. You, more than anyone else, should realize that. The raiders won't come in peaceably. They are not afraid of us, Frank. To them, the Army is trying to tear down their way of life, and they don't like it. That's how you got your legs, Frank, or don't you remember?" His voice was level and controlled. Turning back to the chair, he stooped to retrieve his hat from the floor.

"Wait a minute, Trent." He waved a packet of papers at him. It was twenty years since the Fall, and the Army was still trying to run on paper.

"I have a proposition for you." He talked fast, trying to hold Trent's attention. "All the particulars are in these sheets. These are letters of authority, signed by me. Who to contact, stuff like that."

Trent wheeled to look at the Colonel. "Letters of authority for what?"

"There's a situation west of here, about sixty miles. Big lake area in the Ozarks. It's a place called Big Springs. They have a good thing going out there. The place is starting to grow and has its own economy. Do you realize how important that is? They're raising their own food, making their clothes, running two grist mills so they can grind grain and another one to saw lumber. They are not dependent on anyone. Unfortunately, raiders are also terrorizing them. The name Pagan Reeves keeps popping up. He may be the head snake or just working for Jeremiah Starking. We don't know. I need you to find out."

"You mean scout the situation, and report back." Trent was skeptical and showed it. Taking the sheets of paper, scanning the information. "Why doesn't the Army take care of this? That's right up their alley. The exercise would do them good."

Frank stood up, looking seriously at him. John was his oldest courier. He was also one of his closest friends, yelling and screaming aside. "John, civilization is gaining a foothold. That news flash may have passed you by. You are making people nervous around here. My superiors think you're getting a little wild for the present locale." He smiled grimly. "Besides, most of my men are busy guarding the pack trains coming out of the cities. They can't be spared."

"So what's the deal?"

He eyed his friend with the same scrutiny he'd give a live grenade. "I have a commission for you."

"I don't want to be an officer in your damned army," Trent said levelly.

"Not that kind of commission."

———————

TRENT SMILED a little as he saw the Colonel was about to the end of his patience.

"We're reinstating the office of the United States Marshal. I want you to be the first charter member." Bonham reached into a drawer, pulled out an object, and tossed it on the desk in front of Trent.

The object on the desk was a five-pointed star, surrounded by a smooth silver circle. In the center, the inscription, *US Marshal.*

"What's this, Frank, a bull's-eye?"

"Take it, John. It's about the only job I'm going to have for you." There was just a hint of pleading in the Colonel's voice.

He sighed and held the Colonel's gaze. "Nope."

"What?"

"I'm done, Frank. I'm tired, and I don't want to do it. Do you know there are parts of the country where I can go and not see anyone for months? Months, Frank. That sounds good to me. Real good."

At that moment, the door to the office swung open,

and the girl that had been waiting outside strode into the office.

Offering her hand to an astonished Colonel Bonham, she said, "I'm Katherine Stephens...call me Katie."

She turned to Trent. "Hello, again." Her voice smoothed out, became soft and throaty. She had changed into different clothes, jeans, and shirt, and he was right about her hair. It fell to her waist.

She reached out and softly caressed his side. "How's the wound?"

He felt heat start at his collar and work its way upward, as Frank looked suspiciously between the two of them.

"I decided to call you Katherine."

Katie looked at him, momentarily nonplussed. Regaining her composure, she turned back to the man behind the desk.

"Colonel," she said. "I need to talk to you."

"Well, since you invited yourself in...please, have a seat."

The two men looked quizzically at each other, mentally shrugging their shoulders.

"I couldn't help overhearing you mention Big Springs. That is where I am from." It looked like she was getting ready to launch a long story, so Trent found another chair, turned it around backward so he could lean his forearms on the back, thumbed his hat back off his forehead, and settled in. Even if he didn't like the story, he could always just watch the girl.

"I have some pack animals with supplies that I need to get to Big Springs. I had hoped to hire some men to help, but so far, there haven't been any takers. Colonel, I need an escort."

"You realize, Ms. Stephens, we are not in the business of escorting settlers around the country." Colonel Bonham had regained his patience.

"I know that, Colonel. I also know you are sending out training patrols for your *Green Jeans*."

The Colonel grimaced at the analogy.

"It would be a simple matter for you to send a squad along as a training mission." She turned her persuasive eyes on the Colonel and smiled.

Trent sat with the chair tilted back on two legs, grinning at Frank and enjoying his discomfort. The man looked like he wanted to take up field work again. Soon.

"How did you know that?"

"There are not many secrets around here, Colonel." She turned and faced Trent. "And now for you, *Mr. Trent.*" At her intensity, he nearly lost his balance on the teetering chair. "You told the Colonel you wouldn't take the job of Marshal?"

At Trent's cautious nod, she continued. Her voice was soft and insistent, harboring a sudden, deeply suppressed anger. "Have you forgotten the body of the girl you found? Remember Markie? Is your memory so short? Who is going to right *that* wrong? Who will find the person that could *do* that kind of thing and then disappear into thin air? Who?"

She paused for breath, scooting her chair around to face him. She placed her hands on his knees, her gaze intent on his face. "I've been asking around, talking to folks. People will talk to you, John. People from both sides. They know and respect you. They'll listen to you. No one else but *you* could walk into a raider camp and come out alive. The settlers that are still alive, still functioning out in the frontier, need you."

"It'll be dangerous." Frank, ever the tactician, sensed an advantage and teamed up with the girl. "There won't be any courts out there and no military backup. Just you and that damned six-gun you like to wear. You could take your time, John. Weed it out, get the right of it, and then don't waste my time with reports. Any action taken will be by you, on your own authority. Do you understand that, John? Do what needs to be done."

He'd read a story once about the old Texas Rangers. One crisis—one ranger. Maybe it was the way. "I always have, Frank." He turned to Katie. "What makes you think people are ready for the law?"

She answered promptly. "Because that's what makes a community work. Rules. So people don't step all over each other."

He stared at both of them momentarily. "All right. I'll do it. However, understand this. I'll do it my way." He looked at Katie. "I was going back anyway, Katherine. That's one wrong I intend to right."

The two men shook hands, their eyes lingering on each other. Each knew the risks and the dangers. The handshake was a long embrace between two friends.

Frank sat back in his chair, studying the situation. "All right, here's the deal, young lady. You get a squad. They will take you as near as possible to Big Springs and then return here. You are lucky one of our more seasoned sergeants is in camp." He paused for effect. "You'll also get our number one US Marshal as scout for the trip."

The chair legs hit the floor with a sharp bang. "Frank."

"What better way for you to get into the area?"

Katie rose from her chair, a pleased look on her face.

"We leave in the morning." She looked pointedly at Trent. "First light."

Frank was shaking his head. "How old are you, Ms. Stephens? Aren't you kind of young to be running around the forest alone?"

"How old do you have to be?" She paused, holding each of their eyes for a moment, and then quietly closed the door on her way out.

"Wow." Frank's voice was admiring.

"I think we've been had, and it only took her about thirty seconds."

"No shit," came Frank's garrulous reply. "But it was kinda fun."

He raised his hand as Trent started to leave. "Son."

Frank's voice had changed. The only time Frank had called him son was when his daughter was killed. He cleared his throat. "We need to talk…"

———

THE SUN WAS SETTING in a golden hue behind silver-rimmed clouds looming in the west. A breeze had found the grassy knoll that stood sentinel duty above the mass graveyard in the field below. John Trent hadn't wanted to bury his young wife in the common graves, so he picked a quiet place that was surrounded with boulders and trees, and had a thick carpet of grass and prairie flowers. He laid her to rest over a year ago. Now, finally, he knew the truth about how she died.

He was just starting to leave when he heard footsteps behind him.

"Katherine."

"You got good ears."

Trent shook his head. "You walk soft enough."

She moved around to the other side of the grave, sitting on a chair-sized rock and gazing intently at him. Finally, she asked, "Did you love her?"

"I don't know. Maybe. We were young. We needed each other. That was enough for us. She didn't deserve what she got."

"You blame yourself."

"If I'd been there, it wouldn't have happened." His shoulders slumped with a force he didn't know if he could lift.

"You can't know that. Look at me, John." When he didn't respond, she upped the ante. "Please?" Finally getting his attention, she continued. "Women aren't help-less. We're not all fancy playthings in lace and bows that have to be protected all the time. Some of us actually do things by ourselves, with no help from anyone else. Sometimes we have to stay by ourselves. It's been that way since the first farmer took his wife west to the Promised Land. It'll be that way until the end of the earth. So, it's nonsense to think that you are to blame. The only one to blame is the one who did it."

"Did I tell you she was the Colonel's daughter?"

She sounded confused, with a small dash of concern. "No. You skipped that part. Does it make a difference?"

"He was the one who found her." Their gaze locked for a moment then parted.

"Okay...and?"

"He just told me she died like the girl we found in the clearing."

She was silent for a moment. Then... "God, I am so sorry."

It was nearly dark, and she moved over by him. Her hand was like a burning brand on his arm, and he felt uncomfortable sitting by his wife's grave with another woman.

"Do you think she would like me?"

He laughed and surprised himself. Laughing was something he hadn't done in quite a while.

"Oh, no. No way. She'd be jealous as hell."

She leaned her head against his shoulder. "Maybe. Maybe, not. I'll tell you something, though. If she were still alive, I'd take you away from her."

He looked at her quizzically.

"You were cheating yourselves, John. Needed each other? Maybe? Probably? That's not enough. You need love. Passion. You need that fire in your belly that you can't get rid of, your senses full of each other. Nothing else matters. If you love someone like that, you won't even see anyone else."

He breathed in the scent of her. "That doesn't come along very often."

"True enough. What did you feel when we were in the clearing? And what about the second time? When you found me bathing in the pool, I damn near fainted. I can't believe you didn't feel the same connection."

"We'd better go, Katherine."

As they stood, she was suddenly in his arms, holding his head with her hands and burning him with a kiss that stopped time in its tracks. When she released him, both were panting and he couldn't take his eyes from her lips.

Her voice was soft as her blue eyes dueled with his gray. "Why don't you see if you can get *that* out of your belly." She moved her hand downward and chuckled.

"Well, at least you want me. We can't discount that. It's important, too."

After she left, he stood in the darkness and couldn't complete a single thought. *Damn.*

SIX

THE GRAY LIGHT of dawn found Trent at the holding area, just outside of base camp. He'd been up before daylight, packing his gear, and cleaning his weapons. This trip, he was traveling light, so there wasn't much to get ready, just some dried jerky for times he couldn't hunt, a bedroll and ammunition. It would be enough.

Settling in under a tree, he leaned back against the trunk. He didn't worry about the pack train getting by him. They had to leave camp in this direction, so the unit would probably form up around here somewhere. He automatically scanned the area, saw nothing of interest, then pulled his hat down over his eyes and went to sleep.

A few minutes later, the first of the trainees arrived. The soldiers were in full battle rattle, carrying at least sixty pounds per man, their packs piled high on their backs. They had pots on their heads, and clunky boots on their feet. Trent did not have to open his eyes to know exactly where each one of them stood. There was the usual complaining and grumbling. Some stomped around asking foolish questions of other men who didn't know any more than they did.

He could hear the comments of some of the men who kept looking over at him. Apparently they weren't impressed. Dressed in jeans with buckskin leggings and shirt, and a brown bush hat that had seen better days, he didn't dress to impress. Some commented to each other about his single-action revolver in a land of semi-automatics and his lack of equipment. None came close enough to bother him.

"All right, fall in." A new voice. The voice of authority. He opened his eyes and sat up. That was a voice he knew.

"Gunny?"

The grizzled sergeant turned with a surprised look on his face and strode toward him. The men shook hands, each staring at the other.

"Been a while, Gunny."

"It's been that. Heard you went down last year. Something up at Caplinger Mills?" The eyes of Gunnery Sergeant Melbourne Thomas were brooding and penetrating, his face, after the initial surprise, lacking expression.

"It was a near thing." He was puzzled. Where he expected a more animated reunion, all he got in response was a perfunctory and lukewarm greeting. And the reunion was short-lived.

"Sergeant." Another voice of authority had entered the arena. He decided at once that there were too many voices of authority around here.

Gunny turned, waving indolently at him. "Over here, Lieutenant."

"Better get them together, Sergeant Thomas. We're

ready to move out." He looked distastefully at Trent. "Is this our scout?" His voice left the impression that he hoped it wasn't. "Why don't we have Army scouts?"

He stepped forward. "John Trent, Lieutenant. I'll be going with you, and I know the country. So does she..." He heard the packhorses coming toward them, so he just pointed his thumb back over his shoulder. "I don't think you'll get lost."

"Very well, Trent. I am Lieutenant Spencer. You'll take orders from me, and I've already been briefed on the woman." He turned briskly to Gunny. "Sergeant, we'll move out in thirty minutes. I'd like to meet with Miss Stephens, you, and the scout in fifteen. We'll have a troop meeting in twenty. Understood?" Not waiting for a reply, he walked off in the direction of Katie's pack train.

"Nice guy, huh?" He stood with his thumbs hooked in his belt.

Gunny didn't reply, just turned and walked off while Trent looked after him with troubled eyes.

"This is going to be a fun trip. I can tell."

———

FIFTEEN MINUTES LATER, they were standing under the same tree. The pack train was waiting, and the trainees were standing at ease, at least as much as they could with a sixty-pound pack strapped to their backs, sweltering in the heat.

"There are a few things I want to get straight before we leave." The lieutenant's eyes riveted both men. "Chain of command. I'm in charge of this training mission. You both take orders from me. Is that understood?"

The sergeant's affirmative reply dwindled into nothing as Gunny looked at Trent's retreating back.

"Who gave you permission to leave, Mr. Trent?" Lieutenant Spencer's voice thundered.

Katie grimaced, knowing the type of man Trent was, and already angry at this idiot lieutenant. Gunny just rolled his eyes as he saw Trent stop, hesitate a moment, then slowly retrace his steps.

He stopped with his nose about an inch from Lieutenant Spencer's face. His voice was purposefully soft. He knew how important it was to keep the trainees from losing faith in their commanding officer. "Spencer, I'm going to say this just once. First, you have no authority over me. I'm a United States Marshal. New, to be sure, but it's your superiors who gave me that authority. Now, I've been around the park a few times, Lieutenant, and you will *not* run over me. If push comes to shove, according to the articles in my pack signed by Colonel Bonham, you are to assist me."

Gunny was quietly trying to insert himself between the two men.

"Second," he continued. "I am leaving this group and going my own way, Lieutenant Spencer, because you are a walking dead man. The only chance you have for survival in these hills is to do everything your sergeant says, when he says, and how he says. Then, if your stupid arrogance doesn't get everyone killed first, you just might have a chance of coming back. Third, you didn't have brains enough to get horses and pack animals for your men. Sure, they can walk it, they're tough kids. That's not the point. You need to make time, and your men need to be fresh in case you come up against raiders. And, Lieutenant, you *will* come up against raiders. The fourth thing is this." His voice got deadly quiet. "If you ever yell at me in that tone of voice again, I will piss on your campfire and ruin your whole day. Now, is that clear?"

The lieutenant tried to respond. "I'm a lieutenant in the..."

"Shove it, Lieutenant," he said flatly. "No one cares." As he left, he brushed by Katie. She reached out and caught his arm.

"John, please don't go. I need you."

He stopped reluctantly, not wanting her to see his anger. "Why? You've got Lieutenant Green Jeans."

"Do you remember those men you had trouble with, the ones who were outside Charley's place? They came this morning and offered to herd my pack animals. When I turned them down, they didn't like it much. John, I can smell raider a mile away. So can you. You know they'll hit us on the trail, somewhere down the line. It's just a matter of when."

He stood, weighing the possibilities. None were any good, and he realized she was right. He could imagine what Hobbs's men would do if she hired them. They would have gone with the pack train, and then when the time was right, tried to take it over. Since that ploy didn't work out for them, they'd be waiting up in the hills somewhere in ambush, just looking for their chance. A show of force might just keep them away.

"What's in your packs?"

She looked at him steadily. "Ammo, food and medicine—and toilet paper. Just everything any self-respecting raider would kill for." She chuckled a moment. "I did *not* know they'd figured out how to make that again."

With an exasperated sigh and softly uttered oath, he

turned back to the small group who waited for his decision. "Gunny, there's a good place to camp about twenty miles east of here. On your map, it's the junction of 'U' highway and Eleven Point Creek, in grid fourteen. I will see you there tomorrow if you push hard, otherwise I will see you whenever you make it. I'm going to make a side trip first." At Katie's questioning look, he said innocently, "I'm going to the library."

———

KATIE LOOKED after the lieutenant as the man stalked off. He'd just received the worst tongue-lashing he would ever be likely to get. And it was well deserved. Now, she figured his men were going to get one, too, if for no other reason than for the lieutenant to let off steam. She almost felt sorry for the man. Almost.

She went to check on her pack animals. They carried a valuable cargo—one she wasn't supposed to be bringing back to Big Springs. Her thought was to get in and out of the camp without anyone paying attention. People come and go all the time. Now, she was worried. Those men had scared her more than she wanted to admit. What worried her more was how easily they'd given up. Maybe they figured to have the cargo anyway?

As she finished the chores, she stood, hands on hips, gazing after Trent. The library?

SEVEN

JOHN TRENT WAS NATURALLY CURIOUS —ALWAYS had been. He liked to know things, especially information about the country he was in. It was no surprise his thoughts wandered about the origins of the pathways in the Ozark Mountains.

Before the Appalachian Mountains were heaved upward in the Paleozoic ages, the Ozark Mountains were there. Before the Rocky Mountains were home to the dinosaurs in the Laramide years, the Ozarks were there. The soft contours and rolling forested slopes give way to rugged highlands that have been a mystery since man had time to wonder.

Millions of years ago, sand deposited on beaches of ancient seas became sandstone that lay buried under layers of limestone, left by the receding water. As the world changed and evolved, eons of ice, rain, and wind wore away portions of the soft sandstone, leaving a valley of elephant-sized rocks, and deep, cool canyons with craggy overhangs of rock and trees.

At the headwaters of Eleven Point Creek is a large

spring that comes bubbling out of a little cave about halfway up a medium-sized mountain. Cascading through layers of limestone rock, dropping into sandstone pools, then escaping back onto limestone ledges again, the stream finally comes to rest at the foot of the mountain, forming a pool of clear, cold water about a hundred feet across.

Three sides of the pool sported a dense growth of forest fern and arrow weed. Honeysuckle leaned its branches over into the water, while honeybees worked the sickly-sweet blossoms for pollen.

The fourth side of the pool is a gravel bar, where the water finally escapes its rock-lined boundaries and tumbles onward down the brush-choked valley to join with other tributaries to become a medium-sized stream.

It was the second day that he'd been waiting for the pack train, and the third day out of base camp. He'd scouted ahead of them, snooping through some of the obvious places an ambush might be staged. He didn't really think the raiders would strike this early, but you never knew. They weren't stupid and were completely unpredictable. He thought an attack would come a few days from now when the soldiers would be tired and irritable. Their fatigue would cause them to cut corners to save time, and the soldiers would have trouble staying awake at night while they guarded the camp. If it were to happen, that's when the raiders would strike.

Sitting with his back to a boulder the size of a house, he was cooking a noonday squirrel over a hat-full of fire when the pack train ambled toward the clearing. He'd been hearing them for the last ten minutes, and marveled that they marched up a rocky wash, advertising their existence to all who wanted to hear. They could as easily be traveling on the soft earth next to it. He reminded himself to ask Gunny about it. The sergeant should know better.

He could see the lieutenant leading his men up the wash, with Katie and her pack animals bringing up the rear. As he watched, she raised her hand in a half-salute.

Slowly the party of pack animals and soldiers moved into the clearing. The lieutenant came straight toward Trent's small fire. Looking past him, he could see the men were dead on their feet. Leave it to the Ozark terrain to take the starch out of you.

Katie, with the help of a couple of soldiers, hazed her animals toward a grassy clearing nearby. Gunny was missing.

Lieutenant Spencer stood looking at him a moment. Unconcerned, he turned the squirrel over the fire, browning it as it turned. The juices dripped into the fire, making a sizzling sound that brought rumbles of hunger from the watching soldier.

"We're late." Lieutenant Spencer did not sound as authoritative as he had three days ago.

"Yes, you are." Standing up, he glanced at the squad of soldiers. None had taken off their packs. They were waiting for orders, a plus for discipline but not much for common sense.

"Lieutenant, if you'll take some advice, I think you should camp here until tomorrow. Your men look done in. You could use the opportunity to check them out on camp procedures, defensive positions, that kind of thing."

Lieutenant Spencer sighed. "I think you're right, Trent." He turned and made a hand sign to the men. With relieved groans and grumbles, the squad dropped their packs and went about their tasks with efficient movements and purpose.

Catching Katie's attention as she finished hobbling her horses, he motioned her over to his fire. The lieutenant sat on a rock nearby. "Where's Gunny, Lieutenant?"

"We saw some smoke yesterday evening. I sent the sergeant to investigate. He told me he would pull a cold camp and catch up with us this morning." He gazed back down the trail. "He's overdue." Lieutenant Spencer looked at him. "Why?"

"I just wondered. You know, Spencer, you shouldn't travel in creek beds. I know it's easier sometimes, but sound travels a long way in these canyons. I could hear you coming for nearly a mile."

As Katie came up to the fire, he pulled a wooden plate from his pack, cut the squirrel in half, and shared with her. Digging into the ashes at the side of the fire, he produced two brown trout wrapped in leaves that were baking in the coals. Putting one on the plate, he passed the food wordlessly over to her.

"If you're trying to get on my good side, you've made a good start." Her strong white teeth were already tearing the meat apart, eating with her fingers.

The lieutenant looked at her portion, then at Trent's, and got up to leave. He could take a hint.

Trent moved about his part of the camp, putting out the fire, cleaning utensils, and stowing away his gear. Katie was unashamedly licking her fingers as she used them to clean the last of the grease from the wooden plate. Her eyes hadn't left him since she came to the camp, a fact that made him more apprehensive by the minute.

"Why?" he finally asked.

She didn't act very surprised. "What?"

"Why are you watching me all the time?"

Katie let her gaze wander over him a moment—long enough to make him uncomfortable. "I like to watch you. You don't waste any movement, are sure-handed and quiet. I like that." She grinned at him as she held the wooden plate out to him. "You're also going to make some lucky woman one hell of a good cook."

He smiled a little as he bent to take the plate. "I'm just used to doing for myself." He looked at her pointedly. "That's something you should consider. I've been doing for myself a long time. I'm set in my ways. Likely, some younger man might be better for you. After all, I am probably twice your age."

"You trying to get rid of me?"

His smile was slow in coming. "Now, that would be plain crazy on my part. I just want to lay it out so there are no misunderstandings." His face slowly colored up under her frank scrutiny.

"You are worried, aren't you?" She laughed, then held her hand over her mouth to suppress a grin. "Are you afraid I'm going to get"—she searched for the right word —"amorous?"

"You do that here, you'll get spanked." He tried to be serious, but it was a losing battle.

"See," she said with dancing eyes. "That's what I like about you older men. You have more imagination."

"And just how many older men have you had?"

He wasn't ready for her serious answer. "None...yet."

He laughed and changed the subject. "Did you have any trouble coming up the trail?"

"No, none to speak of," Katie said soberly. "But I got some brewing here."

As he raised his eyebrows, she hooked a thumb over her shoulder, pointing at the soldiers. "One of the Green Jeans has been staring at me a lot. He even tried to talk to me a couple of times. I think he's working up to something, and I'm going to be the main attraction."

"Need me to speak to him?" Trent asked softly, looking over at the men.

"Nope. I am a big girl. I will handle it. Of course, you might stay close..."

He nodded as he walked off to see the lieutenant, leaving Katie to stew in her own juices.

EIGHT

THIS ONE SCREAMED. *She was tough and strong, and he hadn't meant to do this again—not this soon. But there she was, and she was young and pretty, her shiny black hair pinned into a bun in the back, and she looked scrubbed and clean, and the virginal innocence was an aura around her...and he could not stop.*

She was fast—he had to run her down, and her long black skirt kept tripping her, making her easy prey. Even then, she almost got away. She struggled and fought and lost the funny little white cap she wore on her hair, the lace soiled with dirt and grass stains. He stuffed it in her mouth to shut her up. Finally, he tied her to the stakes he hammered into the ground, smiling at her reassuringly. He pulled flint and tinder from his pouch and started a little fire. With reverence and gentleness, he placed the end of the small branding iron in the fire, the one with the cross on it that would become cherry red in moments.

Pulling up his pants a few minutes later, he looked at her scornfully. She'd stopped crying, and her black eyes followed him everywhere he went. Just like the other, she enjoyed it.

Contemptuously, he pulled out his hunting knife. Eyes wide in terror, she started panting and screaming, her mouth a red rictus of pain

———

THE GELDING MOVED RESTLESSLY under Trent as he sat in a clearing in the forest, considering his options. Lieutenant Spencer had casually mentioned that Gunny was overdue, and then promptly ignored the situation. You don't leave a man behind, not in this country, so Trent had left immediately to back trail the squad of soldiers, hoping to run into the missing man. Following the trail was easy, at least until now.

The soft earth in the clearing showed tracks of more than one band of horses, making any sign impossible to find. It looked like a regular parade of people had gone through this clearing since morning. Over one track, he saw a wet, brown spot. He could picture the native hill people stopping to look at the tracks, gazing after the patrol, probably shifting their cud of chewing tobacco from one cheek to the other, then spitting a long brown stream at the tracks. Their contempt shown, they would disappear back into the forest. *One thing was certain. The patrol was not fooling anyone.* By nightfall, the news would be all over the hills. They might as well have brought a brass band with them.

Seen from the last ridge he crossed, a small cluster of buildings nestled at the bottom of the next hill. He turned his horse that way. Gunny was probably there, swilling moonshine, telling lies, and sampling the local women.

Topping a small rise in the dirt road, he reined in the gelding. The small hamlet spread out before him, a few rundown buildings on both sides of the path they called a road, or more likely, in this part of the country, they called it a trace. No one was visible along the street, not surprising considering the heat.

Sweat trickled down his sides as he took off his hat and ran fingers through his hair. Drying his hands on his shirt, he slipped the loop off his revolver and pulled the AK from its boot on the saddle. Clucking to the horse, he rode down to the buildings.

The slow-walking gelding was tense as a spring as he neared the largest of the buildings. Muscles bunching and nostrils flaring, the horse came to a stop in front of the only building sporting a sign. Ziler's Mercantile. Holding his AK in one hand, he was starting to climb down off the horse when a voice startled him from behind.

"Better not."

The level of suppressed anger in the voice spoke reams about what would happen if he didn't obey. The tone surpassed any language barriers.

Several doors along the walk began to disgorge a ragged band of people, mostly women and kids. Glancing behind him, he found the men. They were all armed, and looked to be ready for target practice, with him as the bull's-eye. His rifle was in his right hand. Swing and fire it? Fatally slow. To draw and fire his pistol, he would have to shift the rifle, or drop it. They had him. Stone cold.

Let's see you talk yourself out of this.

He turned in the saddle to confront the men. Most were just holding weapons, not pointed in any particular direction. The sallow-faced young man standing in front of the group was pointing his double-barreled twelve gauge right at Trent's middle. *Persuasive.*

"What's the problem?" Trent asked, just to get something going.

"Like you don't know?" The barrel of the shotgun came up a bit.

"I don't, or I wouldn't ask." He was more relaxed now that he had gotten a better look at the man's weapon. He knew he could draw and shoot before the man pulled the trigger on the shotgun. It was an old piece with individual hammers for each barrel, and the man hadn't cocked either one. The man could fire by pulling the triggers, but that was a hard pull. The fraction of a second it took would cost the man his life, if it came to that.

"What are you doing around these parts?"

"Passing through…" He spoke reasonably, needing desperately to defuse the situation. "…looking for someone."

"I think you're lying," the man shouted and brandished his shotgun.

He was trying hard to think of a reply that wouldn't result in a shooting, when another voice broke in—an old voice, but one still strong with vitality.

"Let him go, Lon."

"He's a stranger, Gran. I bet he's one of them *raiders* we keep hearing about."

"Don't matter, Lon. Use your head. If he done it, he wouldn't ride back into town, right down the middle of the trace. Don't be stupid." The woman spoke evenly, but it was obvious she was used to being obeyed.

Lon looked to be trying to figure out if he'd been called stupid when a gray-headed woman stepped around from behind Trent's horse. Tall and erect, dressed severely in black and gray, she was the matriarch of the clan. Her eyes were sharp and bright. *Anything less than the truth told to this woman would reap nothing but grief and pain.*

"Let's start over, mister. You can see we're a little upset. What's your name?"

"John Trent, ma'am."

Her expression said she'd just bitten down on something sour. "Don't try to butter me, boy. What're you doing here? We ain't exactly on the main trail."

He laid it out for her. Who he was traveling with and why, and who he was looking for. Several of the men nodded when he mentioned the Army patrol. "I used to be a courier for the Army. Right now, I am a brand spankin' new US Marshal, headed for Big Springs."

At the mention of being a marshal, several people smiled, and most of the crowd nurtured looks of derision on their faces. Even the kids thought it was funny, no doubt raised with stories of moonshiners and the law. Their mistrust of the law was inherent in their genes— from way, way back.

"These hills ain't been too kind to lawmen, as a general rule. However, times are different now. Everything's different." Gran stopped and gazed at him, lost in thought for a moment. Coming to a decision, she spoke forcefully so everyone could hear. "Might be we could use some law, now and again. We've had some trouble and don't know how to fix it. Why don't you climb off that horse and see."

Walking into the mercantile, she turned at the door and addressed the crowd. "Y'all go on about your business. Lon, set some of the men to keep watch. We'll be out later."

He followed the woman into the building. What she called trouble lay on a wooden bench at the back of the room. The form looked like a woman. He had no doubt that it was. The blanket was too short to cover all of the body, so they had covered her head, letting the feet show. Her left foot still had on a black lace-up shoe. *Homemade.* The other foot was bare and bloody—both had rope burns on the ankles. He shook his head. *Another killing. What the hell?*

The old woman seemed frailer now that she wasn't in front of the townspeople. Authority is a heavy burden. She didn't make any effort to approach the body. Her voice was old gravel, washed in mud and loathing. "Sometimes I think I've been on this earth too long. It's time for me to go." She shook her head. "But I can't...my people...?" She straightened her back, and he could see the effort it took. "Someone killed one of our girls. Did things to her." Her voice broke and her eyes pinned him. "We tried to trail whoever did it. The trail just petered out and went away. Left just enough for us to think it's maybe one person, and a man."

Anger colored her voice. "There ain't many people we can't trail in the woods, mister brand spankin' new marshal. You know anything about this?"

"More than I want to. There have been others."

The old woman kept silent for a few moments as she digested this, searching his face with eyes that had seen more pain than they should ever have to see. With a catch in her voice, she said, "She was the prettiest girl here. We were hoping to marry her off soon."

"Gran," he said softly. "I don't mean any disrespect,

Lord knows I don't. But I need to look at her. All of her. I have to know if she was killed the same as the others. You know...not just that she died, but exactly *how* she was killed." He inclined his head toward the door. "I wouldn't like to get shot while I'm doing it."

"She's naked."

"Yes, ma'am." He nodded, waiting for her decision.

Finally... "Will it make a difference?"

"Truthfully, I don't know. And it's surely not something I look forward to. I've seen enough dead people to last a lifetime." Trent sighed and met her gaze. Her eyes were red with unshed tears. "I'm kind of new at this."

She looked at him with a little humor peeking around her grief. "My god, an honest man. You'll never last." Then... "Go ahead, Marshal. I'd appreciate it if you don't touch her."

Understanding the stubborn pride and moral code these hill people possessed, he said simply, "Of course."

Leaving the building a few minutes later, he paused outside the door and took in a deep breath. The girl looked much the same. Maybe a little more hurried in the handiwork, and he needed to think about that some. Her belly sliced open, her pubic hair scalped, and the nipples were gone from her breasts. And the brand. What significance a cross burned into her forehead had to anything, he didn't know. There was a lot he did not know. *Too damn many questions. Not enough answers. I hate this job already.*

The old woman was waiting, watering his horse from a bucket, flanked by several men and women. Even in the heat, the men all wore bib overalls and long-sleeved homemade shirts. Black hats and full beards on the men, bonnets on the women, firmly seated in the last century.

Not an old, rusted-out vehicle anywhere. They probably never had one, or needed it.

"Well?" All eyes were on him as Gran asked the question.

He addressed them all. "Counting this girl, there have been three women killed in this particular manner that I know of. There may be more...probably are. I don't have a clue about who did it except he, or she, is very good in the forest. They obviously have a small branding iron and a very sharp knife. There hasn't been a sign left anywhere to look at."

He saw a few of the men look at each other, nodding. He knew they'd tried to trail the killer, and their failure rankled.

"That's all I know."

One of the men spoke up around his cud of tobacco. "That ain't much. How you going to keep this from happening again, Lawman?"

Trent answered truthfully. "I can't. You know that, as well as I do. Before the Fall, there were hundreds of thousands of lawmen, maybe a million. Even back then, the law couldn't protect you from something like this. It's no different now. Evil has a mind of its own. You have to take care of yourselves, people, just like you've always done."

"Well now, that's a right big help."

Trent smiled ruefully. "I know it isn't much, but it's all I can tell you. For my part, I'll do my best. That's the only promise I can give. Meanwhile, you protect your womenfolk. Keep your eyes open. Don't let them go anywhere without someone with them. I don't think this killer likes a crowd. I also think it's a man, from the one heel print I saw. He's strong and a woodsman.

There is one other thing. If there's any doubt, shoot to kill."

"We 'bout shot you, mister." The laconic reply came from one of the older men.

He looked pointedly at the man. "That's why I rode down the middle of the street. So there would be no misunderstandings." Addressing all of them, he said, "I know it's a couple of days' travel, but if you need me for anything or find anything I need to know, I'll be at Big Springs."

As he mounted and started to leave, the old woman had a final comment. "You got a badge, lawman?"

"Yeah, somewhere," he answered, searching his pockets.

"Better pin it on...might save you from any..." She hesitated a moment. "Misunderstandin's."

He reached into his saddlebag and found the badge, and pinned it on his shirt. "You might have a point there, Gran."

One thing he'd forgotten to mention to Gran and her folks. Tent pegs. Hardly anyone pitched a tent anymore. Who in hell had tent pegs? Heading back up the trail toward the standing rocks of Eleven Point Creek, he remembered his original mission—*where in the hell was Gunny?*

———

IT WAS NEARING TWILIGHT when Trent rode up to the campsite. The sound of the water bubbling over the rocks had muffled his approach, and he rode unannounced right into trouble.

Katie had backed up against a rock, the campfire

between her and one of the soldiers. Wide and muscular, he was already moving around the fire toward her when Trent's voice came to him. "Soldier, I'd like to save your life."

The big man whirled. "What'd you say?"

"You heard me. Now get back to your own part of the camp."

"Or you'll do what?" The soldier was half Trent's age, and held a short machine pistol, barrel pointing down.

"I'll kill you." He said it simply.

The soldier looked at him full of contempt. "I got an automatic in my hand and your toy pistol is in its holster. Now, I am no hotshot courier like you, but I just have to believe I got the edge here. I think you're dead meat. As a matter of fact, I think go ahead and I'll kill you first, and then enjoy your woman the rest of the night."

"To do that, you'll have to be able to pull the trigger."

The man stood facing him. "Aw, I heard of you. You are supposed to be some 'quick draw' artist, like Wyatt Earp or sumpin'. I never believed those old stories, and I don't believe you."

"Then kill me."

The big soldier looked at him calmly standing in front of him, and suddenly started to sweat. A minute ago, he was sure he could kill the man, but now the seeds of doubt were starting to sprout in his brain. To make it worse, the other soldiers were watching. There wasn't any way he could back down. He was going to have to try it. Slowly, the barrel of the machine pistol started coming up.

"Benson, get out of there." Gunny's voice was bull-horn loud, blasting over the sounds of the river like a pounding fist. Walking up to the soldier, Gunny repeated,

"Move, soldier, or I'll be taking a personal interest in makin' you suffer."

Benson's eyes shuffled between Trent and Gunny. Grumbling, he finally sidled away toward his side of the camp.

He spoke levelly to the sergeant. "That was close."

"Ah, hell," Gunny grumbled. "You probably shoulda' just shot him. Save one of us the trouble later."

The lieutenant coming over to them, his boots scrunching in the gravel, interrupted their conversation. "What's the trouble, Sergeant?"

Trent answered for him. "Your man Benson was out of line, Lieutenant. I also couldn't help but notice you sitting over there doing nothing about it."

"Sergeant? I was talking to you."

He glanced at Trent before he answered. "I'll take care of it, sir."

The lieutenant looked across the fire at Katie. "Very well. I don't think the..." He paused and looked her up and down. "...lady was in any actual danger."

Trent's fist cracked against the lieutenant's jaw, lifting him off his feet, and the man's shoulders made a crunching sound as he hit the gravel. Oblivious to the cocking of weapons all over the camp, he reached down and jerked the lieutenant to his feet. Holding the wobbly-legged man upright, he breathed a soft warning to him. "Don't you ever speak to her in that tone, Lieutenant. Not ever. Is that clear?"

Gunny took over. "Benson, get back over here and take the lieutenant to his bedroll. He must have tripped on something over here. The rest of you men go back to whatever useless things you were doing. Stanton and Ashe, take first guard. Move it."

Coming back, Gunny said to him, "Must be the humidity. Tempers are kinda short around here, and me not even having chow yet." He looked pointedly at him. "You'd do well to get that girl out of here. She's trouble, even if it's not her fault."

He'd been thinking the same thing and grumped at himself for leaving her with the soldiers. He walked over to her. "Are you alright?"

"Sure. I can take care of myself, you know. I'm not helpless. That really wasn't necessary."

He ignored the bravado, his eyes full of concern for her. He reached out and brushed her hair from her face. "From now on, don't get so far from your weapon. Don't ever go unarmed. Even when you think you're among friends, or if it's just a call of nature. It might make the difference."

She smiled and batted her eyes at him. "Yes, father."

"And don't be a smartass." He couldn't help but smile.

"And don't you be so protective of it. I've decided it is already yours." She seemed to love watching him turn red.

He pondered that with a smile on his face while he sat down to talk with Gunny.

"I heard you were out looking for me?" Gunny said.

Trent's gaze pinned his friend for a moment. For a fleeting instant, he wondered about that. They knew each other. Friends might be going too far. "We thought you might be lost."

Gunny looked at him seriously. "No point in looking for me, boy. There'll never be a day you could find me out there. You should know that."

He watched as Gunny abruptly got up and walked away. *Now what was that all about?*

―――――

KATIE AND TRENT lay in their bedrolls on opposite sides of the fire. With their heads close together, their conversation was soft and quiet. He told her about the other killing. She lay mute, thinking about it. Finally... "I don't understand the kind of person that would do that." Her voice was mildly plaintive in the night.

He could understand her problem. Maybe that's why a killer like this is so successful. "I know it's hard to get your head around. I did some reading on it. Even if we do know the type of person that does this, it probably won't put us any closer to catching him."

She abruptly rose up on an elbow. "Wait a minute. You were reading?"

He grinned at her. It was true that many people couldn't read anymore. The only schools were back east or in the few established settlements scattered around the country. "You don't think I can read? Do you remember the side trip I mentioned? I went to the library in one of the abandoned towns we passed. I didn't find much, the place was a shambles, but there were a few books left that didn't go to the local outhouses." He thought for a moment. "Mainly they broke the killings down into four categories; visionary killers—people that hear voices and have visions, mission-oriented—getting rid of a certain group of people, hedonistic killers, couldn't find a dictionary to look that one up—they kill for sexual gratification and usually mutilate the victim, and the power-oriented killer—they like to control and dominate."

"This guy may fit all four," came her musing reply.

"I know," he said around a yawn. "But we'll find him. One way or another."

Katie was already asleep. Great, his explanation put her to sleep. Bet she wasn't the only one to sleep through that class. He stared at the stars, showing through the hole in the canopy of trees above them, for a long time. Once, he saw a shadow moving away from them between the boulders. There was nothing to hear.

NINE

THE PREDAWN LIGHT slowly appeared as a white envelope of humidity and fog. Cooler air had moved in during the night, and the dense growth and damp ground gave up its moisture in surreal fingers slowly lifting toward the canopy of leaves above. Water dripped from the leaves, shaken loose by a few twittering sparrows grumping sleepily at the new day.

The tree-covered hilltops were seeing the tip of the sun as it came up, but the valleys between the hills remained shrouded in the gloom of shadow and night.

John Trent came awake with instant awareness, listening to the sounds of the forest as he opened his eyes. Something was wrong.

With awareness came action, and he silently snaked out of his blanket into the darker shadow of the huge boulder next to him. Breathing shallowly, with his mouth open to give his ears a better chance at hearing, he strained his senses into the dawn.

Turning slightly, he looked at Katherine lying a few feet away and saw that her eyes were open and staring at him. He made a slight hand motion, and after a startled glance around, she slowly started moving toward him. Once she gained the shadows, she quickly came to him. He hadn't realized she slept with her rifle, something he needed to file away for future reference.

Without taking his eyes off the forest, he pointed toward one of the sentries. Slumped over a rock, his posture could easily have been mistaken for slumber.

"What's wrong?" Her breath was soft and warm in his ear, and he heard the nervousness in her voice. He hoped she wouldn't panic, but suspected there was a lot of iron in this girl.

"His gun is missing." He looked across the clearing and could barely make out the sleeping patrol. Gunny had spread his blankets away from his men, around a bend in the clearing. Trent hoped he was awake. He reached out and pulled Katie to him as his hand unconsciously caressed her hair. His senses filled with her as he whispered. "Raiders. They're inside the perimeter."

With hand signals, he had her cover the clearing to the left. He would take the right.

Trent thought of tossing a rock into the sleeping men, hoping to wake them, but he was too late. Someone tossed something else.

A serrated, round object bounced once with a metallic click on the rocky floor of the clearing.

"Is that a...?" Her astonished voice echoed loudly between the rocks, but the indiscretion didn't matter. Nothing would matter in about three seconds.

"Down." He hurled his body into hers, dumping her to the ground behind a boulder.

They heard the thump and roar of the explosion at the same time metal shrapnel and shredded rocks hit the boulder they were behind. Close behind came the sound of automatic weapons. Ears ringing, he rose from behind a waist-high rock and began firing. Rushing bodies and gunfire filled the camp. The sleeping squad of soldiers leaped from their bedrolls after the grenade went off and lost three men to gunfire before they went back to earth.

During a sudden lull in the firing, he heard someone screaming. He vaguely remembered seeing a wounded man dragged out of the camp and into the brush. The screaming abruptly stopped.

Again, the firing picked up. He reached for his pack of extra magazines for the AK. He saw Katie grimly shuck out a spent magazine, and slap in her last spare, never taking her eyes off the clearing.

"Let's show them we're still here." His voice was level and cool. As she came to join him, he raked the perimeter of the forest, his assault rifle firing as fast as he could pull the trigger, Katie's AK-90 roared on full auto.

Suddenly the clearing was full of rushing figures as the raiders charged their position. Katie's rifle was empty again, and she was trying to find another magazine as three men darted toward them. The action of his rifle clacked open, and not having the time to reload, he palmed his pistol, dropping two raiders as they came around the boulder. She pulled her small Browning .380 from her ankle holster and shot the third raider just as he was lining his sights on Trent. She then turned and expended the rest of the sixteen-round mag at the retreating backs of the fleeing raiders.

Wordlessly, Trent handed her a magazine for her AK-90 and covered her while she reloaded. Snapping it in, she jacked back the charging handle and was ready, eyes wide with adrenaline and trying to look everywhere at once.

As suddenly as it started, the attack was over. The silence following the brief battle was deafening. Immediately reloading his rifle, he positioned Katie between two rocks and slipped into the forest. Single shots punctuated the morning each time he found a wounded raider.

Gunny and Trent walked into the camp from opposite sides, stopping suddenly as they caught sight of each other. Katie straightened with an audible sigh of relief. The surviving soldiers began drifting out of whatever cover they had found during the brief fight.

Gunny's anger was scathing. "Look at them. These soldiers are really something." Taking a big private by the arm, the same one who had given Katie trouble, he asked, "Where's your weapon, Benson?" The wild-eyed man was looking vainly for his MAC-10. "Where's your damned weapon?"

"That's enough, Sergeant." The lieutenant came walking up, brushing leaves and dirt from his uniform.

Gunny whirled around. "Enough? Christ, it's not near enough. Not one round fired, Lieutenant. Not a single damned one. These recruits scattered like a bunch of kids. If it hadn't been for Trent and this girl catching them by surprise, we'd all be dead."

"We didn't do so bad." The lieutenant's voice had a plaintive edge to it. "It could have been worse."

Walking toward Katie, Trent spoke as he went by. "Just where is your rifle, Lieutenant? You lost three men plus your two sentries. That is five. Our horses are all gone, plus the pack train. They got what they wanted. The only reason they attacked was to keep us busy. They got it all. All the supplies and ammo you have left is whatever is in your packs. I call that damn near a disaster." Coming to Katie, he said softly so only she could hear, "Pack our gear. We are leaving."

She didn't waste time arguing, just turned and began throwing their things together, knowing he wanted to keep watch on the forest. She was done in moments.

He turned to the soldiers. "You're on your own, Gunny. We're pulling out."

The lieutenant blurted, "You can't leave us, Trent. The Colonel said you were to guide us."

Ignoring him, Trent spoke to Gunny. "We're drawing too much attention. This crowd is too big. You'd do better to break into small groups and scatter. The raiders know you are here. They'll be nipping at your heels the rest of the way home. We're going to use that to our advantage and just fade into the trees while they're watching you. Katie can take me into Big Springs."

"I will have to stay with them." Gunny's voice was regretful as he looked at the remaining men of the patrol.

"Watch your ass, Gunny." Trent held his hand out and the two men shook.

Glancing around the clearing, littered with bodies and the smell of death, Gunny replied, "Yeah, I hear that."

"Ready, John." Her voice was subdued, but her chin was up and her eyes steady. The smell of cordite was heavy in the moisture-laden air, and the morning sun was already promising the oppression of another hot day.

Leaving the clearing, Gunny's voice followed them.

"Trent? If I don't get fragged bottle feeding these damned killers, I'll come by to see you."

"You are welcome anytime, Gunny."

———

MIDMORNING FOUND them on a bluff overlooking the river. They were still following Eleven Point Creek, and Trent knew they would have to turn away from the river soon, to head northeast toward the Current River and Big Springs.

They were walking in a pine forest. The needles on the floor of the forest muffled all sound of their passing, and the whispering breeze hissing through the trees at the top of the bluff was soothing and cool on their faces.

He dropped his pack to the shady floor of the forest and stretched, looking out over the hills and valleys.

Glancing back, he noticed Katie sitting on her pack, arms around her knees, just staring at the ground. She hadn't said much since the attack earlier that morning, and now, as she sat there, she started to tremble and shake. The aftermath was starting to set in.

Kneeling, he wrapped her up in his arms, holding her head to his shoulder.

"It's all right, Katherine. Your body is just reacting to losing all that adrenaline. The shakes are normal."

He handed her his canteen, and she gratefully put it to her lips. She'd never known her mouth could be so dry. "Do you get the shakes, too?"

His expression softened. "Sure, but I usually do it late at night when no one can see. I have to protect my image." His hand stroked her hair and his voice was gentle. "Your first time?"

"Yeah." The one word was full of emotion.

"You did good." He could see she didn't believe him. With no idea of her upbringing, he didn't have a starting point to help her. It was beyond his comprehension that she'd be so isolated that she never saw anything like that.

"Did I? Really? I killed some of those men. I've never

killed a man before." Her voice was a mixture of loathing and wonder.

He roughly pulled away, hands still on her shoulders. His eyes held steadily to hers until he was sure she was through feeling sorry for herself. He watched it all march past in her eyes. Loathing. Despair. No one should ever have to kill. It was not fair.

Slowly, then, reality set in with her knowledge of the real world. Then resolve. But not pride. She was not proud of it, but she knew deep down that the killing was unavoidable. It was simply the price of survival.

The hands that had roughly held her away from him started caressing her arms and shoulders.

His voice was gentle. "How did you do today? Let me evaluate you as I would a soldier, Katherine. Most important of all, you were quiet and didn't ask stupid questions. You did what I asked you to do without hesitation, and yes...you had the guts to kill when you had to. There was no choice. Those people who attacked our camp weren't going to stop and let us take a vote about whether we wanted to die, and they sure as hell weren't going to debate the morality of the situation. They were going to kill you. Or worse. Or both. Remember that."

He continued. "Look at how the recruits did. They ran like rabbits. If more of them were like you...they might not have lost so many men. Besides..." He finished with a humorous glint in his eye, trying to get her mind off the attack. "You even saved my tail. That last raider would have put lead into me if you hadn't nailed him."

She smiled slightly at him, her eyes burning with something he'd seen in her before when they met at the clearing.

"Then you owe me. Right? There's bound to be a code of the forest or something like that? You're in my debt?"

He looked at her and eased away, not sure where this was going. "I suppose..."

"Then pay up."

A half-formed question was on his lips, but it just made things easier. Her lips found his, softly clinging, then grinding with hunger. Her arms went around him as she entwined her fingers in his hair and held him against her.

"Are you sure about this?" Part of him wanted to slow down, the other part called him an idiot.

Her answer was another kiss, this one softer and full of promise.

All his resistance to her, which wasn't much in the first place, fell away as his hands cupped her buttocks and pulled her tight against him, crushing her breasts against his chest.

Breathing heavily, she broke the kiss, chuckling as his mouth found her throat and his hands worked on the laces of her shirt. "Why, Marshal," she breathed. "The things you do...and right here in broad daylight."

TEN

THE FOLLOWING day found them high on a mountain overlooking a natural basin about two miles across. Although he couldn't see it from their vantage point, Trent could hear the rumble of water erupting from the huge spring below.

He gestured at the basin. "How did all this come about, Katherine? I had it pictured in my mind as being a lot bigger."

She dropped her pack to the ground and came to stand by him, gladly taking on the role of tour guide just to get some rest. He hadn't stopped all morning, and her tail was dragging.

"You hear all that noise from below? That's the spring. I found some old tourist brochures that the Conservation Department put out before the Fall that told all about it. Millions of gallons of cold, clear water comes bustin' out from under this mountain every day. Then it makes a river of its own for about two miles, then ducks into a cave and disappears. It finally ends up feeding into the Currant River."

He stood with his hands on his hips and took a deep breath, taking in the cool, moist air coming up from below. Katie came to stand in front of him, fitting into him naturally.

If this was to be his base of operations, he needed to know all about it and didn't relish finding another library. "That's what started the settlement, then? The water?"

"Yep. There were some small towns nearby, but when the plague started, no one knew what caused the sickness. People were scared. Some of the locals thought contaminated water caused the plague, so they holed up here in the basin. This water was the cleanest around, I guess. At least, it was clean enough that the people didn't die. Of course, there weren't many people here until the last few years."

"How did they keep everyone out? I would think once the word got around, everyone would want to come."

"You'd remember this more than I. Anything us young folk know is just hearsay." She arched an eyebrow at him. "But with people dying so fast, it was pure panic. Not many thought of Big Springs, and a lot that did, died before they got here. Then, of course, there was the road."

"Road?"

"There was only one road into this place, so they blasted it out. All this limestone is soft. A few sticks of dynamite in the right spot made the road disappear under a few tons of rock. Now the only way in or out is game trails, on foot or horseback. Those can be watched if need be."

She was staring into the basin, leaning against him, absentmindedly rubbing the back of his hands that he'd locked around her.

His thoughts turned to their lovemaking the day

before. He didn't know why he felt contented and apprehensive at the same time. Maybe things were too good to be true. "Katherine, about yesterday."

She leaned back into him, pushing with her buttocks. "What about yesterday? You feel you were cheated or something? Got took advantage of? Don't like pushy girls? What?"

He sighed and shook his head. "Be serious."

She twisted around to look him in the eyes. "I am dead serious."

When you're alone as much as he, expressing thoughts to someone comes hard. His mind stuttered and started a few times, and he was sure his mouth was opening and closing like a land-locked trout before his lame reply finally spilled out. "I just want you to be sure, that's all. I'm no bargain."

"That's a matter of opinion, Old Man," she said with a chuckle. "I'm not some city girl from back east looking to climb the social register or go to some cotillion. Wait, are there enough people to even do that anymore? What I'm trying to say is you are exactly what I want and need. Clear?" She picked up her pack. "Come on. We go around this bend, and you can see the town."

A few minutes later found her staring in awe at the settlement. "Where did all...?" Her voice faded with the question. "There was nothing like this when I left."

He pulled a pair of binoculars from his pack. Focusing the instrument pulled a vision of the town right up to his nose. The settlement had one street, with buildings lining each side. A few houses randomly dotted the basin floor, and off to one side stood a small country church, complete with steeple and bell tower.

The single street, lined with men lounging around,

horses and wagons tied to rails and posts, was a well of inactivity. No one seemed to be doing anything. Then, while they watched, a group of men erupted from one of the buildings. They saw the puff of smoke long before they heard the insignificant sound of the shot. The group turned and trooped back into the building. The one left on the ground didn't move.

His expression turned grim. "Looks like you've got a lot of new residents. Not too friendly, either."

"Raider?" She still watched the village below in undisguised disbelief and kept shaking her head.

He just shrugged. He couldn't tell from this distance. "Raider, mercenaries, survivors, who knows? Doesn't make much difference what you call them. They may tell you one thing, but it's what they do that puts the stamp on them."

She'd finally found her own set of binoculars. "I don't see any of the locals, and I can't figure how they got those wagons in. It really is hard to do, or at least—it was." Making a sudden decision, she started down the pine-needled trail skirting the basin. "There is a ranch a couple miles from here. Connie Sanchez runs it. She's a friend of mine and has a bunch of riders out of old Mexico. They are all descendants of the Maya. Nobody messes with them. Connie keeps her ear to the ground. She'll know what's going on."

As he hustled to keep up, he wondered how many more twists and turns there'd be to his new tenure as marshal. And if this Connie person feeds people.

———

THE SANCHEZ RANCH lay in a narrow valley next to the Big Springs basin. The land here was not quite as rough, with the forest broken by small glades and clearings full of grass. In the distance, Trent could see cattle grazing on a plateau, and on another were horses. All of the herds of animals had guards. Someone was very smart. Cattle represented food. Horses represented transportation. Anyone controlling a herd of cattle, or the horses for that matter, could have about anything they wanted. Provided they could hold it. Coming out on a wider trail that led to the main house, a low bungalow with a red-tiled roof and wraparound porch, they hitched up their packs and started toward it.

"Hold it."

The voice had come from the side, next to a giant outcropping of limestone, and Trent silently cursed himself for not being more careful. From the way Katie acted, he thought they might be more welcome at her friend's ranch.

The man who rode around the rock was lean and dark. Both hands handled his rifle as he guided his horse with his knees. His wide-brimmed hat sat on the back of his head, revealing shiny black hair. Smoke from a small, black cigarillo made his eyes squint at them, but Trent doubted he missed anything. This man looked to be all tough whang-leather and sharp spurs. There was no doubt about the M-16 carbine pointed at them.

"You have business here?" The voice was soft and musical, with no trace of an accent.

Katie spoke up, flustered. "You must be new here. I'm a friend of Consuelo's."

Motioning them forward with his free hand, the rifle didn't waver. His voice was polite and calm. Despite himself, Trent was impressed. "That we shall see. Today is not a good day for visitors."

"What about our weapons? We'll not be giving them up." Trent's voice was firm.

The man just shrugged and motioned them on. He had no doubt this man could take down them both if trouble was offered.

"Have you had trouble?" he wondered aloud as he looked around the clearing.

"Each day has its own." The brusque reply was both philosophical and grim as the man followed them toward the house.

As they neared the long porch that circled the house, a woman came bursting through the door. Long black hair framed black snapping eyes and the low-cut dress revealed her dusky complexion. Short and voluptuous, her dress trimmed in jewelry, she looked more like an Indian princess than a Mexican landowner.

"Katie," the woman exclaimed as she hugged the tall blonde girl. "Welcome back. We were so worried."

"How's it going, Connie?"

Consuelo's dancing eyes sobered a moment as she held her friend at arm's length. "It goes. How do you like my new foreman?"

"He seems very capable." Katie smirked at her. "And very handsome."

Trent was watching the retreating man on the horse and was thinking of joining him when Connie turned to him. "And who is your very handsome man?"

Katie pulled him by the arm as they moved toward chairs on the porch. "Connie, this is John Trent." She waited for the name to sink in. It didn't.

"How do you do?" The black-haired beauty let her

eyes roam over him from head to foot. Her Mexican accent was suddenly thick as syrup. "I am the Contessa Maria Consuelo Gonzales Pelenque y Sanchez. You are most welcome to my home."

He didn't know whether to doff his hat, bow from the waist, or fire a twenty-one-gun salute. Lacking the proper guns and not knowing the protocol, he compromised. "Damn!"

"That's what I said the first time." The new voice came from within the house. "Of course I've been here a lot, so I'm used to it."

The door behind them opened, and a big man eased himself onto the porch. The truculent voice and mocking eyes set warning bells off in Trent's head. Slowly, his hand went from his belt to resting on his pistol. The loop over the hammer was already off. His gaze met Katie's, looking for direction. Somehow, she had led them into a nest of snakes, and he decided to walk softly, not wanting to step on the wrong one. Her eyes were on Consuelo, and he suddenly realized what had happened. He'd been in the woods way too long.

Consuelo was obviously flirting with him, Katie was gearing up for an old-fashioned clawing match, and another man was staking out the Mexican girl as his own territory, leaving Trent in the middle. This was just too damned complicated.

The man had stopped and was staring at him. "I know you."

"I doubt it," Trent replied evenly, watching the man like he'd watch a cranky copperhead. "And you are?"

"Pagan Reeves."

The man said it as if the name was supposed to mean something. There was something about him that made Trent want to reach out and slap him. "I know the name, can't say it's nice to make your acquaintance." This was one of the men Colonel Bonham talked about. Brutal and ruthless, Reeves was supposed to have no side but his own. The two men stood, staring at one another.

Katie couldn't keep the news to herself. Pulling Consuelo to a table, they sat as she dropped the bombshell. "John is a United States Marshal."

"A marshal." At first, the Mexican girl was unimpressed, and then confusion took over. "Like, a lawman marshal?"

"The Army assigned him to Big Springs to keep the peace and sort out the troubles." Katie continued, seemingly oblivious to all the side play.

"Alone?" Consuelo said in incredulous tones as she shuttled her gaze between Katie and Trent. "Have you seen the town since you have returned?" All trace of an accent was gone. "There are at least fifty mercenaries in town alone. They have just about run all the honest people off. We hear there is a big-cheese raider camped out in the hills, just waiting for everyone to clear out so he can move his families in. We need an army here, not one man."

A little stung by the lack of confidence, he moved off the porch. "Well, I guess I'll just have to make do."

The contemptuous voice of Pagan Reeves followed him. "You won't last a day." Reeves stood with his hand close to his holstered pistol. "I remember you now. You're the Army courier. Scout. Supposed to be a real tough man."

Reeves's mocking voice was pushing it and Trent didn't want anything to happen here because of the women. Too many get hurt in shootouts, and not necessarily the people doing the shooting.

"You'll be dead in a day." Reeves continued taunting him. "Maybe I should just save the boys in town the trouble and run you off right now."

Coldly angry, he turned suddenly. With his earlier caution gone, he faced Reeves. "Why don't you do that? You run me off. Do it right now. You have a fancy auto-loader pistol and probably have at least fourteen shots to my six. Come on. Use it."

Their eyes locked, and he kept getting closer. Finally, they were facing each other with less than a foot of space between them. "How about it, Reeves? You gonna pull that shooter?"

Pagan Reeves was sweating. Any gunplay now would get them both killed. Neither could miss. He was desperately looking for a way out when a stern voice interrupted them.

"Enough of this."

Moving into his line of vision, Trent saw the man who had escorted them to the house. He was holding a large bore Smith and Wesson as if it were part of his body. He pointed it at Pagan.

"Sure, anything you say, Chico," Pagan said immediately, trying to regain some of his bravado. He backed off slowly, trying to leave the impression he was reluctant to move. Looking maliciously at Trent, he mounted his horse. "Trent. You come to town, and you'll die. Big Springs is mine. I have the town and the men to hold it. But you come on ahead, Marshal. You just come on."

Reeves whirled his horse and rode away in a cloud of insignificant threats and dusty bravado. He was gone in seconds flat.

Trent turned to face the Mexican, the pieces of his memory finally clicking together. "Chico Cruz."

The man slightly inclined his head as he holstered his pistol. "The same."

"I have heard many things of Chico Cruz," Trent said evenly, his gaze trying to match up what he'd heard with what he saw.

Chico grinned at him. "And I have heard of the courier, John Trent."

Katie broke in. "If this mutual admiration society could break up, it's time we left. It's getting dark, John."

"Alright, Katherine."

"John?" Consuelo had walked up to them. "John, is it? And Katherine? He calls you Katherine?" She looked at Katie, who was turning several shades of red, holding her hand to her mouth. "Now I see. I'm so sorry, Katie. Now I know why you were getting so mad." Connie giggled softly in her hand. "Please, both of you. Stay with me tonight."

Katie shrugged her shoulders. It was impossible to stay mad at Consuelo. "All right, we'll stay, if it's alright with John." He nodded, strangely pleased that she asked but wasn't surprised that she never stopped talking. "Let's go inside, Connie. We have some catching up to do."

"Why was Reeves here?" His abrupt voice threw the question out for anyone to answer. He was examining puzzle pieces, and none of them fit.

Consuelo turned and regarded him for a moment. "It's very simple. He wants me." Her gaze held his. "He wants my land...he wants my cattle. Mostly, he just wants. Up to now, it's been easier to put him off and humor him than to fight him." She looked over at Cruz with a troubled gaze, and he thought her eyes softened a little. "We may have to fight him now."

After the women went inside, Cruz turned to him. "He is a dangerous man, this Reeves."

"He's got some yellow in him." He was trying to come up with any information on Reeves, other than what the Colonel told him, and came up blank.

"Yes, but he's all the more dangerous for it. With him, you have to watch your back."

He finally breached the question that had been burning inside him. "Last I heard, you were Jeremiah Starking's second in command. Your name is on every Army bulletin board in the territory." He smiled at Chico. "All, two or three of them."

The humorous glint in his eyes belied his serious words. "So. Do you now challenge me, Marshal Trent? We have always been on opposite sides, my friend, but we know of each other and are very much alike, I think. There would be no gain for either of us if we fight."

He shook his head. "Sometimes there is no gain. I've been given a job, Chico. It's a thankless one, but like the village idiot—I took it. Now, I wear a badge. That doesn't impress anyone yet, but I've been thinking about it and I like the idea. It's a job that needs to be done if people are to survive. I decided I'm going to do the job that goes with the badge. If I do it well, then the badge will gain respect. If I can do this, then the next man to wear the badge will have respect. I may not have a choice where you are concerned."

"There are always choices, my friend." Cruz scraped a line in the dust with his boot. "See? Between us is a line. You are on one side. I am on the other. What separates us, Trent? You have killed. I have killed. Now, suddenly, you have a badge. Do you now think your killings are somehow official? If you decide someone should die, you will perform your duty. There are no questions asked. If I decide someone is to die and kill them, I am a criminal and a murderer. I am wrong simply because I don't have a badge. My question for you is this? Does the badge make you right, Trent? Or is this badge simply the horse you ride to get what you want?" Chico Cruz stood straight in the evening sunlight, a tall man burned brown by the sun. "Don't show your badge to me and expect me to honor it. I won't. But I'll honor the man and judge you by your actions."

Both men had turned and were leaning against the fence railing of the corral. Trent watched as the horses nipped and played in the evening coolness, thinking of what Cruz said. The problem was Trent liked this man, and of course, he was right. He respected him as one fighting man does another. All he had ever heard about Chico Cruz was that he was a tough man in any kind of fight and never a word about senseless killings or brutality. But he had been Starking's righthand man. And Starking was a raider. Was his opinion of Starking wrong, too?

Here, standing in the approaching gloom of evening, in a ranch yard he'd never seen before, he felt he'd found a kindred soul. Both men understood each other, as can only happen when the same ground has been covered, the same battles fought. Each had tasted the blood and dirt of their wins and losses.

He took his time. He wanted Cruz to understand. "Chico, ever since I joined the Army, I was about seventeen, I guess, I always tried to do the right thing. I have a deep feeling for what is right. I guess we can call it the law. Not laws written by legislators and congressmen, hell, they're all dead anyway, that are written on a whim and can't be enforced. There's an older law. The one most people are born with."

"From the first-time man sprung from the well of life, he has had a sense of right and wrong. Someone must stand up against those that take advantage of weaker people. I guess that's where I've always tried to be."

"But now, you have a disadvantage." Cruz flipped the stub of the cigarillo into the corral. "Now that you have the badge, and if you honor it, you must be right, and just. Above all, you must be sure. Sure of your position and what you do. You must be all these things before you pull your gun, my friend."

"So, you think I should throw the badge away." He looked quizzically at Cruz.

The man shrugged eloquently. "The man on the other side of this line we talk of, like Pagan Reeves...has no decisions to make about right or wrong. He knows exactly where he is. And he knows where you are, and won't hesitate or be bothered with doubts. That gives him the advantage, because you'll always have to wait that extra second until you know. Until you are sure. The other man doesn't care if he is right or not." He reached over and tapped the butt of Trent's pistol. "When that time comes, you will have to be very fast, my friend, and very, very good."

"Which side of this line are you on, Chico?"

He thought for a moment. "For each man and each circumstance, I must draw the line." As Trent raised his eyebrows, Cruz continued. "You wonder about this. We cannot always be brave. We cannot even be right all the time. To survive, we must deal with each situation by itself. My job is to protect the Senora Sanchez, and preserve her rancho. This I will do."

"Then if I yell for help...none will come."

"I heard about the fight at Caplinger Mills. There were six men? I don't think you will need much help."

"Maybe." He smiled ruefully at the man. "And maybe I bit off more than I can chew."

———

THE WATCHER SAT *in the shade of an old incense Cedar that was twisted and gnarled with age. The shady blanket of needles kept the setting sun from reflecting on the glass of his binoculars.*

The women below him, brought into sharp relief by the ten-power lens, were beautiful, full-breasted, full of life and vigor. But no, he would have to look somewhere else. These women are worthy but too well-guarded. The pistolero would guard the Mexican girl and guard her well. The blond-haired woman was with Trent and the Watcher did not want to antagonize Trent. At least, not yet. His eyes went back to the blonde woman. He watched her walk across to the corral below and felt the heat stirring within him. She was beautiful. He knew she would be soft in places she needed to be. Would her nipples be large and soft, or small and hard? Her skin would be tight, and part like...he forced his eyes from her. Maybe later. It would be fun...later.

ELEVEN

BIG SPRINGS WAS BUILT on either side of the old Conservation Department access road that entered the small basin between the hills. Mills populated the part of the road that paralleled the springs, using the rushing water to power their huge paddlewheels, which turned the gears and grinders that processed corn and wheat, or turned the blades for sawing lumber. Across the old and broken tarmac were buildings that housed a trading store and meeting hall. A few houses and a church were at the south end, and a lone building used as a tavern was on the north.

As he made his midmorning ride into town, he thought about the best way to handle this new situation. He'd dressed with care, wearing jeans and knee-length moccasins, a blue cotton shirt with his new star pinned on the front, in plain view. His rifle was in its boot, and his right hand rested on his hip, near his gun. Sitting tall in the saddle, he rode down the middle of the street toward the tavern.

He'd discussed his reason for coming alone with Cruz last night.

"At least let me go in with you in the morning," Cruz argued vehemently. "My riders can watch your back for you."

"Thought you didn't want to help," he replied chidingly. "I'll go alone, Chico. If we go in with a show of force, there'll be a fight for sure. If I go alone, maybe they won't be so jumpy. I could use the loan of a horse, though."

In the end, Cruz agreed, and the horse he gave Trent was magnificent. Too large to be a good cattle horse, the sorrel gelding reminded him of stories of the Mexican Conquistador's horses they rode into battle. *A battle horse. Fitting.*

He could do all the planning and figuring he wanted, but when faced with a problem, he only knew one way to solve it. Straight on...don't pull your punches, and the devil take the hindmost.

Chairs lined the porch of the saloon, most of them filled with men he assumed were mercs, and hangers-on, the likes you would find in most any settlement. The local spit-whittle-and-chew club.

He cataloged them as he stepped down from his horse. They'd be bad as a group, but he didn't see anyone that might be trouble by himself.

"Morning," he said as he took the front steps two at a time. He held a rolled-up piece of cardboard that he'd taken from the back of his saddle. "Who runs this place?"

One of the mercs turned his head and spat a brown stream into the street. "Who wants to know?"

Without breaking stride, Trent reached out with a toe and kicked the front of the chair out from under the man.

The merc flipped over backward with a crash, his head cracking against the building on the way down. A look of dumb surprise washed over his face.

"I do." Trent stood waiting as if he didn't give a damn what the merc did, and in truth, he didn't.

Finally, when the man saw no one rushing to his rescue, he muttered, "Murdock runs it."

"Thanks." Turning to one side, he palmed his Ruger, reversed it, and used the butt for a hammer to tack his poster to the wall. He stepped back and surveyed the men on the porch. "Read it. If you can't, find someone to read it for you."

Moving into the gloom of the saloon, he stopped just inside the door to let his eyes adjust to the dim light. This saloon, he no longer thought of it as a tavern, looked different in that it was neater than most. The bar across one end was polished, and the floor swept and clean. He looked around at the men and women sitting at tables and leaning against the bar. Some he knew from other places; some he'd never seen. Still, there weren't any he would call raider. Not yet, anyway.

"I'm looking for Murdock." The noise fell to a whisper when he came in, and his voice carried easily.

A large woman, who looked to be in her late twenties, got up from one of the tables and crossed around behind the bar. Leaning forward on her elbows, she looked him over the way a schoolteacher does the class prankster.

"I'm Murdock." She didn't ask what he wanted or who he was.

He could see now why the place was neater than usual. It had a woman's touch. When he thought of her as "big," he didn't mean fat. This woman was over six feet tall, and proportioned to size. When she leaned forward, her breasts tried to explode from the low-cut dress. In the subdued light, her face was smooth and featureless, her eyes unreadable as obsidian. He vowed to be very careful and not low-rate this woman.

"You run this place?" Trent asked the obvious as he scanned the crowd with his gaze.

"Every inch of it, mister. What'll you have?"

He brought his attention back to her, trying to keep his eyes off her cleavage. "A speech and a beer, in that order."

She grinned at him, and the hardness left her face. "Alright, this should be interesting. You give the speech and I'll get the beer."

He turned and hooked his elbows on the bar. While looking nonchalant, the position actually put his hand closer to his gun. He knew at least one in the room that didn't miss that fact. "My name is John Trent. Some of you know me. If you don't, you will get to. What passes for a government these days will claim I'm a United States Marshal, but you and I know that hasn't meant much in these hills for the last two hundred years. That doesn't matter. You can call me marshal, or law dog, or anything else you want." He shrugged and watched the crowd, trying to not make the mistake of meeting someone's gaze. "None of that matters."

He paused for a moment to let that sink in. The only sound in the room was someone's asthmatic wheeze and the creaking of chairs as people shifted in their seats. "This is what matters. I'm serving notice right now. Anyone not showing some sign of work, or serving some purpose around Big Springs, will leave. It can go easy or hard, and you can have it any way you want. This is a working community. The trouble in this settlement is over."

When there wasn't any comment, he pointed toward the door. "There's a list of people outside on the wall. If your name is on the list, you have until sundown to get out. After that, I'll kill you on sight. Anyone not on the list will have to prove up and be okayed by the people of the town. That's the speech."

He turned and took the beer Murdock handed him. It was cold and beaded with water. He swallowed half the contents before he put the bottle down. "How do you keep it cold?" He kept half his attention on the folks shuffling out the door.

"There's a well in the back that feeds in from the Springs. The water is cold enough to make your teeth hurt." She changed the subject. "Is my name on the list?"

He looked sideways at her. "I didn't know your name when I wrote that up. Besides, looks to me like you have a job."

"I thought maybe you would try to run off all the newcomers and just leave the original settlers."

He hoped a good explanation would make her spread it around to other people. "Nope. That's not my intention. Just run an honest place. When people get too drunk to navigate, send them out the door. If they won't go, send for me. But be warned, I can't be around all the time."

"If they won't go, I'll show them this." Reaching under the bar, she came up with a sawed-off pump shotgun. On the front was an attachment he'd never seen but knew it was called a Duck-bill, a deadly item spawned in the jungles of Vietnam that spread the shot in a horizontal pattern.

"I inherited this from my grandfather. He was a 'Nam

Vet."

He reached out and traced the opening with his finger. "Have you ever used it?"

She grinned at him. "Just once. It was one hell of a sight. A whole bunch of guys came busting in the door. They'd been in earlier and tried to convince me I should be their entertainment for the night. Didn't sound like much fun to me, so I ran them off. When they came back, I let them have it. I don't get many arguments anymore."

He shook his head as he thought of the carnage. "I can imagine. It must have taken days to clean up the mess."

"One more question, Marshal. What about my girls? Do they stay?"

He wasn't aware she ran prostitutes. He idly wondered what they took for pay. "You still don't understand Murdock. I don't have a problem if you're doing normal stuff and not causing trouble. I'm not going to run the oldest profession out of town unless they are spreading disease or rolling drunks and causing trouble. Just keep it clean."

"Well," she said. "I'm not sure the local parson would consider our normal stuff very normal, but I appreciate it just the same."

He noticed her eyes were riveted on the door. Looking around, he saw a cluster of men around the poster he had tacked on the post. One of the men ripped it from the wall and threw it down on the deck.

He sighed and started for the door. "Well, time to go to work."

Murdock called to him. "The big man is the one they brought just for you, Trent. Be careful. He likes to stomp, and he's a nutcracker."

He walked out and straight into the arms of a human bear. *So much for conversation.* As he passed through the door, the man jumped forward and wrapped him up, picking Trent's feet off the porch and trying to break his back. He knew if he didn't end this fight now, he was a dead man. He struggled to free his left arm, his right hand pushing the man's chin back and up. Finally, his arm came free and he cupped his palms and slapped the man on both ears. The first time the man just whined. The second time his grip loosened. When he slipped down in the giant's grasp, he kicked the man on the instep and slid out of his arms. The man howled in pain.

He suddenly found himself propelled into the street and surrounded by a ring of spectators. Most were shouting encouragement to the giant. It was hot and humid, and Trent was fast losing his temper. "Mister, I don't know you, so you'll get one warning. No more of this."

The big man smiled, showing gaped teeth. Blood was trickling from both ears. "The name is Big Waters, lawman, and I am going to kill you with my hands. I'm gonna break you like a stick."

The man was clumsy, but a monster of strength. Trent sighed, knowing he just couldn't chance a long fight, not in this heat. He also knew he couldn't use his gun, or he'd lose what little respect some people might have for him. "All right then, Mr. Waters. Come and get it."

The big man rushed him. When he was an arm's length away, Trent straight-armed his pointed fingers into Water's throat. When the giant lumbered to a stop, gagging for air, Trent slipped sideways and kicked in the man's right knee. With a grinding snap, the leg broke, and the giant went down like a felled tree, screaming and holding his leg. Trent stood looking at the rest of the men and women. "Anyone else?"

The crowd was stunned. Not at the violence, they were used to that. They'd seen men crushed in Big Waters's hands. It was the casualness and quickness. Waters was defeated with no more effort than taking out the garbage. And that was what he intended. He wanted to shock them.

One man dressed in a partial camo uniform spoke up. "Tell it to Pagan Reeves. He will skin you alive."

Trent singled him out. "No. You tell him. Right now." He stared at the man until he turned and left.

"All right, move out of the way." A woman's voice broke in.

He turned to see Murdock pushing her way through the crowd. She was carrying a black bag.

"Jesus, Trent. You should have just killed him." She knelt, looking at the bent leg.

He wasn't sure he wanted to know the answer but asked anyway. "Why?"

"After I set his leg, we'll have to cut down a tree for him to use as a crutch. None of us are big enough to carry him around."

"Use a horse," Trent said solemnly.

————

LATER THAT AFTERNOON, after one of the townsmen found him an empty building to use as an office and place to live, Trent was standing in the empty room wondering what to do with it. A knock on the door saved him.

"Mister?" A young boy was at the door.

"What can I do for you, son?"

"Preacher Stephens wants you to come down to his place for dinner." The towheaded boy stood at the door, trying to see inside.

He opened the door wider. "C'mon in. You got a name?"

"Tommy." The boy shifted from one foot to the other as he looked around. Maybe he was looking for bodies?

He held out his hand. "My name is John, Tommy. Nice to meet you."

Tommy stood looking around, ignoring the outstretched hand. "Not much of a place."

What? "I just got here." He shook his head. "The decorator hasn't arrived yet."

Wrinkling his nose, the boy finally looked at him. "No kiddin'. Know what my dad says?"

Trent raised his eyebrows in question.

The boy rocked up on his toes and then retreated a couple of steps. "He says you got a bull's-eye painted on your butt, and people are goin' to be linin' up soon for target practice."

He grinned at the boy. *Out of the mouths of babes...* "Your father is a wise man."

"My dad says..."

He raised his hand to stop the continuing avalanche of "dad says." "Tommy, you are depressing the hell out of me. Why don't you show me where this Preacher Stephens lives, huh?"

"That's easy, Marshal. Next to the church." The boy left shaking his head, undoubtedly wondering why someone wouldn't know the preacher lived next to his church.

TWELVE

TRENT TIED his horse to the white fence bordering a small white house—a white house that sat next to a white church. *Purity? Doubt it.* He loosened the girth on the saddle and hung on a feedbag.

He unlatched the gate, let it swing shut behind him and walked up to the porch. Looking at the white church again, he thought the whole place looked bleached.

The man who opened the door was a tall, lank man who held himself erect and proud. Although he appeared to be pushing sixty, his hair was as blond as Katie's.

"Reverend Stephens?"

"You must be Marshal Trent." The preacher opened the door, and Trent passed through into a spare room, with a few chairs parked against the walls. An ancient sofa seemed to be the main gathering place in the room. As they stood, sizing each other up, the reverend spoke in a voice meant to carry to the entire congregation. "My daughter seems quite taken with you, Marshal. She talks about you all the time. I'm surprised a man of your age would encourage that."

No beating around the bush here. "Your daughter seems to have a mind of her own, Reverend. She will make up her own mind about who keeps her company."

The man stared at him a moment, then nodded slightly. "Perhaps, she is headstrong. But even strong minds can be changed. How old did you say you were?"

He smiled and replied with icy calm. *Tread lightly.* "I didn't say, Reverend. But since you are asking, I am thirty-six."

The preacher folded his arms across his chest and then turned slightly away. "That would put you about twice my daughter's age, wouldn't it?"

He was beginning to dislike this man. A lot. "Reverend, you are grinding this ax a little thin. If you have got something to say, spit it out."

Katie cut any reply short as she entered from the kitchen. "I see you two have met." She cast an amused glance at him. "I hope you are playing nice."

"Hello, Katherine." Suddenly he was tongue-tied as a schoolboy on his first date. Dressed in a full-skirted dress, with ruffles at the shoulders and a dip in the front that went way below her open-throated tan line, she'd gone from beautiful to breathtaking. He was suddenly aware of his clothes, still dirty from the trail, and the fact he hadn't had a bath in days.

She took him by the arm. "Close your mouth, boy. The flies are gettin' in. You will excuse us, Father?" Not leaving her father any time to disagree, she led him out the back door. "I thought you might want to wash up."

"Thanks for saving me." There was a bench by a well pump with two pans of water. Trent took the hint and stripped off his shirt. She leaned against the side of the house, watching as he washed vigorously in the cold water, and then stood looking around for a towel. Katie reached inside the door, snagged one off a hook, and tossed it to him.

He flattened his wet hair with a comb found on the bench, which made him wish he had a haircut. This, in turn, made him think of his chin and wish he had a razor, which made him wish he were somewhere else entirely. He smelled her before he felt the towel rubbing his back. Lilac and sweetness, mixed with cooking smells of bread and chicken. When he turned, she stepped inside his arms, her breasts nudged up against him, her searching eyes serious and humorous at the same time.

"Don't let my father run over you. It just makes matters worse. We'll have dinner, and then he'll likely preach at you for a while. Then he'll go over to the church to study." She smiled at him. "We'll be alone, then."

"Yes, ma'am." Trent acquiesced with a smile and none-to-gentle squeeze.

"Ah, now. Patience is a good word to think of." Her lips left a small wet spot on his nose, and then she left him to get into his shirt by himself, her fingers leaving feathery tracks down his chest and across his stomach.

———

SUPPER WAS OVER, and the two men were sitting on the front porch. The church and parsonage were set on higher ground, so the valley lay open before them like a mural. Trent tried to remember where he had seen a painting like this. In the distance, they could hear a piano playing in the saloon, or more accurately being beaten into submission—and occasional laughter drifted to them, carried by the summer breeze on its way out of the valley.

The reverend, perhaps trying to circumvent the melancholy atmosphere the evening had brought, didn't waste any time. He waved at the town. "They are a godless people, with little thought for life or propriety."

Knowing this was just another opening salvo, he responded lightly. He could imagine the thoughts of the good Reverend. "Which ones? There are a lot of people down there."

"All of them, Mr. Trent, each and every one of them."

He thought about how to respond to such arrogance. "Well, I'm sure glad I'm not down there."

Reverend Stephens snorted at his sarcasm. "You think you're better, Mr. Trent? I'm not blind or deaf. I've heard of you, and of your kind. Frankly, I can't tell much difference between you and the people you're supposed to protect us from."

He could feel a headache coming on. There were men like this on both sides of any issue. Maybe this marshal thing wouldn't work after all. He wasn't much of a fence straddler. "So your answer to the problem is…?"

The man answered quickly, like he'd given the subject a lot of thought. "Leave, Mr. Trent. The will of God can be done without your assistance. Lives will be saved."

He nodded with a small smile and he tried to meet the man's gaze. "With you interpreting God's will, I suppose."

The reverend ignored the barb. "This killing has to stop. With you here, posing as a US Marshal, the situation will only get worse. No one will have respect for your kind of law. The badge you are wearing is a vain trinket that you should put away. That," he pointed to the worn handle of Trent's pistol, "won't solve anything here."

Trent thought a moment, realizing he and the reverend were at an important juncture. This was a mine-field that needed a careful path. "Has it occurred to you that I may be as much God's instrument as you? When you think about it, we have the same goals. We want an end to the killing, and we want peace." He stood and leaned against a worn post. "Do you think for one moment that your preaching of peace will make any difference to those people down there? They only under-stand one thing. Survival. The quick and strong live. The slow and weak die. They don't want to die, Reverend."

"Violence is never the answer." The reverend was starting to warm up to the subject and he could feel a sermon coming on.

Abruptly, he interrupted the man. "What happens when they come for your daughter? What happens when they decide they want to live in your house? What happens when the raiders become tired of the girls in the saloon, and take after the women in your congregation? How will you stop that, Reverend?"

Stephens did not answer, just turned and looked over the valley.

"I'll tell you, Reverend. Unless the raiders know you will hurt them more than they can hurt you, unless you make the price of their actions so high they won't chance it, then you don't have a chance in hell, Reverend. Not one."

The man turned back to him with a sad look. "And your way, Mr. Trent?"

"You said you've heard of me. Well, so have they. Most of the raiders down there are followers. Oh, they'll kill you quick enough, providing they can get away with it. But most of them don't want to die trying. For those people, my presence will make a difference. That cuts down the numbers and leaves the real problem. Men like Pagan Reeves, and a few others. Those I'll have to defeat, Reverend. There just isn't any other way. I won't have time to debate the issue, or bring them to you for conversion and counseling. The bad ones have tasted blood, and nothing less than blood will stop them."

"And you, Marshal Trent. You've tasted blood. Can you not stop until you have tasted theirs?"

Trent thought for a moment. He hadn't talked at this length...ever. "You may be right. But I'd like to think I'm still a fair man and will listen to reason. Except for one person."

The preacher was thinking of the raiders, and possibly Pagan Reeves, but Trent was thinking of the mysterious killer.

"I'm curious, Mr. Trent. What possessed you to take such a job?"

He snapped back to the present and grinned ruefully at the reverend. "Now, I've thought about that. I have to tell you. If God made me do this, then I wish He had left me alone. My way has always been to let others do as they want, as long as they didn't bother me. Somehow, that isn't good enough anymore. I guess, when it comes right down to it, there just wasn't anyone else around to do the job."

The reverend shook his head. "The Commandment says thou shalt not kill, Mr. Trent."

"See, there you go again, thinking you're the only one who's ever read a book. The original translation in the Greek says thou shalt not commit murder. There's a world of difference in that. It wasn't until modern times that the clergy changed the wording to kill."

"And you think that distinction absolves you from the responsibility of your killing? The premeditation?"

He had to think on that one a moment. The reverend seemed content to wait. Finally... "No, I don't. When you strap on a gun, you strap on the responsibility that goes with it. A gun is a tool used to save lives, as well as take them, Reverend. Your problem is, everything has to be black or white. Unfortunately for you, we live in a world of gray."

"There is only right and wrong, Mr. Trent."

He replied sadly, with genuine regret. He knew that the two of them would never agree. "Then I envy you your clarity, Reverend Stephens, however shortsighted it is."

Both men turned as Katie came out of the house, looking fresh and vibrant. Every time Trent saw her, she looked more beautiful. "I think you two have about beat that subject to death, don't you?"

Reverend Stephens turned to him. "I must go to the church, Mr. Trent, but I want you to know something. I love my daughter very much. I don't want to see her hurt, and I cannot see how you could do anything else."

The reverend smiled. "It's been an experience talking to you."

As he went down the steps, Trent spoke. "When you think about it, Reverend, you may realize we are on the same side."

The man didn't stop walking. "I can't imagine that, Mr. Trent." He continued toward the church, a tall man in a black coat, his back unbending to age—or differing opinion.

As they stood on the porch, Katie studied his face, her eyes dark and serious. "Now this is a side of you I didn't expect. I thought you were eloquent with my father."

"Your father isn't a bad man, Katherine. He just has tunnel vision. Our only difference is a matter of viewpoint."

It was then they heard the yelling. Young Tommy came tearing around the house, cutting under the reins of the horse. The animal reared and nearly broke free from the rail. Trent moved quickly to calm the horse. "Marshal, you got to come quick. Somebody went by the Clark's house, and them people are all dead. The whole bunch of them are dead. Folks are saying it's the plague." Not waiting for a reply, the boy was off and running again, looking for the next place to tell his news.

He sighed and looked at her. "I'd better go, Katie. Most people wouldn't know plague if it bit them on the ass."

"Not without me, you don't. I'll be just a minute."

———

AS TRENT and Katie rode up to the cabin that sat well back in the woods, a small crowd of people gathered in front. Silently they parted to let them through.

He heard someone say the people died of the plague, and he stopped and looked around at them. "Would any of you know plague if you saw it?" Everyone looked at him silently. He could see fear in their eyes, and he wondered why they were here, if they thought the plague had returned. "I want everyone to stay back. You're tromping up the ground where there may be tracks that I need to look at."

Being hill people, this was something they understood, and they backed slowly away.

As he went up the steps, he spoke quietly. "Stay outside, Katie unless I call for you. Let me know if the crowd acts up."

At her nod of assent, he went through the open door. He could see straight through to the kitchen, and saw the bodies. In no hurry to get there, he treated the house as he'd treat a trail he was trying to figure out in the forest.

Quietly, he looked through all the rooms of the small house, his passage known only by an occasional squeaking board in the tongue and grooved floor.

He wandered through a rumpled bedroom full of homemade toys and piles of clothes. The other rooms were in equal disarray, not surprising with small children running about. Long lines of meat hanging on a line adorned the back porch, cut into thin strips and dried for jerky. He paused to smell the meat, thinking it might be a source of trouble. Finally, he stepped from the dirty back porch into the room he'd been avoiding.

All the family was around the kitchen table. He'd purposefully saved this room for last. There was no hurry. It was obvious that they were dead. He was old enough to know something about plague—at least enough to know this wasn't it. Plague takes a while, following the usual course of one person being infected, then spreading it to others. Even the new viral strains that cropped up during the Fall weren't this quick, at least none he'd heard of. Whatever had killed this family had gone full course in a matter of minutes.

Finally, he did what he had put off for so long. He looked at the Clark family individually. Personally. The man and woman were both young and healthy looking.

The woman had fallen forward onto the table, one arm outstretched toward the baby, and the man had fallen out of his chair onto his left side. The baby, about nine months old and sitting in a homemade highchair, looked like it was asleep. He stood there, absently brushing back a lock of wispy hair on the baby's head. At a small noise, he glanced up and saw Katie watching him from the door, tears in her eyes. Looking at the table full of food, he knew it had to be something they ate, or the water they drank. The house was much too drafty to harbor any poisonous fumes or gas, and he knew of no mines around that would produce any noxious gasses. And there were no wounds on them. Seeing a pot of stew on the wood stove formed a question in his mind.

He found the answer in the trash under the sink. Several empty cans of prepared beef stew. The cans were green with corrosion and had to be pre-Fall. How stupid could they have been? The food in those cans was spoiled. He knew from experience the toxin from bacteria growing in food was virulent and quick. They probably just warmed the stew enough to eat and hadn't cooked it long enough to kill the bacteria. He'd seen the same thing in the jungles of Central America. And the same thing here.

"What'd you find?" The voice boomed loudly in the room.

His head cracked against the bottom of the sink. Cursing, rubbing his head, and pushing down the urge to go for his gun—he looked up. "Who let you in, Murdock?"

The big woman held up her black bag. "I go anywhere, Trent."

"Next time, hum a tune or something. You shouldn't

sneak up on a man like that. I've never seen someone so big be so quiet."

"So, what do you think?" she asked, ignoring his complaint and looking around. "Poison?"

He held up a can, careful not to get any of the contents on him. "Botulism."

"Bot...what?"

He straightened to his knees, and a strangely quiet Katie gave him a hand up. "You're some medic, Murdock. Old cans. The food was spoiled."

Her mouth made a round "oh" as he went past her and onto the porch.

"You folks gather around." His quiet voice carried easily in the silence surrounding the house. The people waiting outside shuffled closer. He could see a few mercs in the outer fringes of the crowd. He supposed they were curious. Judging from the number, it looked like most of the honest townspeople were here. He put it to them straight. "The Clarks are dead. All of them. There's no mystery here. The cause is *not* the plague, or anything like it. This is what killed them."

Trent held up one of the old, rusty cans.

"I shouldn't have to be telling you this, especially so long after the Fall. We all use material things made years ago. Material things. It's the way we live. But you can't do that with food, no matter how good it looks, how clean you think it is, or how hungry you are. If you don't grow it, raise it, or kill it yourself, don't eat it. That is survival rule number one, people. Anything you find in cans or jars may be spoiled. When something lays around for years, there is no end to the kinds of sickness it may breed."

He looked over the crowd. "Whatever was in those

cans killed the Clark family in a matter of minutes. You think about that. It just isn't worth the chance. If any of you have food like that stashed away, get rid of it. If you know where this family got these cans of stew—go get the rest and bury them."

Trent paused a moment. "Now, these people need to be buried. Any volunteers?" When several men stepped forward, he turned to Murdock. "You want to take care of this?"

Her green pallor belied her bravado. "Sure, I've seen worse."

He looked at her quizzically, "You got a first name, Murdock?"

The woman looked at him and some color came back to her face. "None you'll ever hear."

Grinning, he left things in her hands and walked back to the horses with Katie.

She looked back at the house. "Sometimes people can be so stupid." Her voice broke. "The baby..."

"Katherine."

"What...?" She turned and saw what had hardened his voice and gave a small gasp.

Pagan Reeves was waiting for him, and it didn't look like a social call. Red Seaver was beside him, grinning widely. The third man was a raider who called himself Tommyknocker. He had two guns strapped to his waist, another in his waistband, and from what he'd heard, a mind totally void of conscience. He'd heard a lot about the Tommyknocker. Mostly that he was insane and mean. Trust Reeves to bring a crowd.

He sighed as he slid the thong off his pistol. "You better stay out of the way, Katherine. I'll be talking to these men."

THIRTEEN

TRENT RODE TO see Pagan Reeves, sidestepping his horse down the hill. His right hand was on his hip, inches from the butt of his pistol, his left-hand shoulder high—holding the horse with a tight rein.

"You looking for me, Marshal?" Pagan's voice was truculent, and he was looking for a fight.

"Not until morning." His eyes never left the three of them. Of the three, he worried about Pagan Reeves the least. He'd run across Red Seaver before and knew him to be deadly with any kind of weapon, but it was Tommyknocker he would watch the closest. The man was wild-eyed and high-strung. If he jumped, no telling which way he'd go.

"Which means...what?"

He could see a small crowd was gathering and felt like Pagan was a test. "Your name is on the list."

"What if we don't wanna' leave?" Tommyknocker spoke in a high-pitched voice as he moved his horse away from the other two.

"Then I'll kill you." He said it matter of fact, with no

bravado or embellishment. It was just a simple statement of truth.

Tommyknocker laughed, and his horse pranced a moment. "You'll never see the day."

He sighed. This had gone on long enough. Better to do this on his terms than hers. "Do you remember the last time I saw you? It was at Caplinger Mills. You were wounded and running like hell."

With an oath, Tommyknocker dropped his hands to his guns.

Trent shot him just below the sternum. He didn't need more than one shot, knowing what hollow points do. As the man slumped, like a puppet with cut strings, Trent moved the barrel of the pistol to cover the other two. Reeves sat in stunned silence while Red Seaver sat cursing under his breath.

"What'd you do that for?" Reeves yelled at him and then watched as Tommyknocker slid from the saddle and his horse skittered away.

He replied in a hard voice. "Never could see talking when it's a shooting matter. You'd do well to remember that. Now, you have a choice. A choice you didn't have a minute ago. Either you can pull that fancy pearl-handled pistol and start shooting, or you can gather your people and leave town. The choice is yours, and I don't have all day. Make up your mind."

Red Seaver said, "Someday it will be you and me, Trent."

"Forget it, Red. It would have to be from the back and you aren't that kind. Besides, I've seen you draw."

"You haven't seen me draw, Trent." Reeves's voice was taunting. "Have you thought of that? I've seen what you can do, and I'm not worried one bit. What do you think of that, lawman?"

He smiled at the man, knowing it would infuriate him. "I saw you start to draw. You just never finished. That's the way people like you are, Reeves. You start, but never finish. You try to get other people to do your killing for you."

Pagan's face turned a mottled red, then faded to gray. When he finally spoke, it was in a choked whisper. "Red, go get the rest of the men. Meet me at Sliding Rock, then we'll go see Starking." He smiled maliciously. "I think open season is about to start on our Mr. Trent."

"Would you care to start now, Reeves?"

Reeves shook his head. "No. I can wait. When the time is right...we'll meet."

Trent relaxed slightly. "It may never come, Reeves."

"Why?"

"I can't imagine ever turning my back on you."

As Trent rode back toward town, he raised his hand in salute to the reverend and Katherine. He wondered where she'd gone. Neither looked very happy.

———

MARSHAL JOHN TRENT lounged in a tipped-back chair that graced the front of his makeshift quarters at Big Springs. Katie had called after him, following the confrontation with Reeves, with a promise to come later and talk. It didn't take much to figure out what the subject would be. He'd even surprised himself with the suddenness of the killing of Tommyknocker. But there simply wasn't time to do anything else.

As he sat watching the few townspeople go about

their evening chores, he tried to collect his thoughts on his first day in town. One minor crisis with the food poisoning and the raider element certainly knew where they stood. His fight with Big Waters had seen to that. Coupled with meeting Katie's father, it had been quite a day. Hopefully, within a few days, the townspeople would start to see him as a help instead of a hindrance. In the meantime, he needed to figure out just how to go about this marshaling job he'd fallen into.

He was about ready to get up and make a circuit through town when he noticed a large man in a floppy hat walk out of Murdock's saloon. His wild hair was barely contained by the hat, and from his appearance, Trent was glad he was upwind from the man. It wasn't his rough appearance that brought his attention, but his manner. The man walked toward him but stopped at a small cabin set slightly back from the street. After furtively looking around, he quickly snatched open the door and ducked inside. In the cool night air, he could clearly hear the sound of a slap and a woman's scream. *What the hell?*

He ejected from his chair and ran to the house. The screaming and cursing continued as he mounted the porch. He quietly turned the knob and let himself in.

The man had the woman backed into a corner, holding her with one hand the other raised to slap her again. As Trent moved toward him, he caught sight of children's faces peering from another room. The man stopped with his hand paused in mid-air when he saw the woman's eyes turn to Trent.

With a curse, the man lunged toward a back door, but Trent's foot intercepted his legs, piling him up on the floor. The woman's assailant came up spitting mad from the floor, but his anger was no match for Trent's cold fury. As the man stepped in, he met him with a straight left jab that crushed the man's nose in a shower of blood. Not giving the man any chance to set himself, he bent him over with a short jab to the ribs and then straightened him up with a solid uppercut to the jaw. Then he grabbed him by the neck and threw him bodily outside into the street.

As the two men came together again, he noticed a small crowd had gathered. The would-be rapist took a wild swing at him that he easily evaded, and then Trent started slapping him, first one hand then the other, until the man was whining in frustration. He drove the man back down the street with his pounding fists.

Finally, he pinned the man against the awning post next to his office. He turned to the crowd who'd followed along. "Someone get me a rope."

"You going to hang him, Marshal? We've all had trouble with that man." The question came from one of the women in the crowd.

He considered the idea a moment. "Well, it's a thought, but I don't think so." Knowing what they were thinking, he held up his hand to avoid an argument. "I know he deserves to be killed for what he tried to do, but that would be over quickly. I have something else in mind."

A few minutes later, he had the man tied to a post with the rope thrown up over a crosspiece, pulling his hands over his head and taking most of his weight off his feet. He stood looking at him a long time as the man groggily looked back. Finally, he turned to the crowd. "Has anyone checked on the woman?"

Murdock pushed her way through the crowd. "She's alright, Marshal. Just scared."

"Good." He turned back to his prisoner. "So, what do we do with vermin like this?"

The comments from the crowd were varied and sudden, ranging from death to emasculation. He noticed a puddle forming under the man that wasn't sweat. "We'll let him hang here all night. The woman he assaulted will have a whip. It's up to her to use it or not. Murdock, in the morning, you can turn him loose. If he's still alive, he can leave town." He turned back to the man. "Mister, I don't want to know your name, where you've come from, or where you are going. If I see you again, I'll beat you to death."

He'd noticed a few men in the outskirts of the group that weren't local—they just weren't dressed right. He directed his comments to them. "The people of this town will not be bothered. Anyone causing problems will answer to me. I won't be giving any more warnings." He was in his office soaking his hands when Katie came in. She leaned on the door as she closed it. There were no lights inside, so he could barely see her in the evening dusk.

"I can't leave you alone for a minute."

He couldn't tell if she was mad or pleased. "Just doing my job...I think."

She didn't acknowledge ambivalence. "What are you doing to your hands?"

"Found some Epsom salts on the shelf. It'll help keep the swelling down."

She stepped forward, looking at his battered hands. "I heard this 'porch ornament' tried to rape that poor woman. Do you think he's the one you're looking for?"

"Not likely. He's too clumsy and not smart enough. No, he's not the one." She came closer, like a forest animal sniffing out something it didn't understand. "What's wrong, Katherine?"

"I don't know—I really don't. You killed a man earlier today while he was just sitting there talking to you. Then, I see what happened out here, and it bothers me. Sometimes, I don't know you, and that scares me. You were so brutal...I have never seen you like that."

He watched her and hoped the dread didn't show in his eyes. Their settlement was unique, and up until now, was safe. Compared to the rest of the country, she'd led a sheltered life. For the first time, he wondered if being with her was just a dream. "You're right. You don't know me, Katherine. I tried to tell you that. I'm not hiding anything from you. This is who I am." He dried his hands and held one out to her. "Come and sit with me. We can talk."

She shook her head, "No. I...I better not. I need to think."

"Then go do your thinking, Katie." His voice was harsh in the gloomy room and he couldn't keep his feelings out of it. "While you're at it, stop by and make sure that piece of filth hanging on the porch is being treated right. Maybe you could take him home with you. I'm sure your father would approve."

He didn't get up to close the door after she left. He wasn't too sure it *would* close after the way she slammed it. Sitting in the darkness, his throat felt raw and his mind empty. He knew his world had just walked out that door. What he didn't know was how to get her back.

FOURTEEN

DAWN HAD BEEN GONE a couple of hours and the midmorning heat pressed a heavy hand on John Trent. The trail written in the bent grass and churned earth turned up by the passage of horses was easily followed. Pagan Reeves and his men had not tried to cover their trail.

He thought back to the night before. His simple ruse had worked. He was sure Reeves was a back-shooter, so he had taunted him until the man went running to the raider chief, Jeremiah Starking. He could have wasted weeks plowing around the hills looking for Starking, but now the trail was like a paved highway, road signs and everything.

Topping a rise, he saw a huge encampment spread out below him. Groups of people milled around the cleared area between at least fifty cookfires. Children ran and whooped through the clearing and farther away, a small herd of horses grazed under the watchful eye of a guard.

There was only one tent in the clearing and he pulled out his binoculars to study the area. Horses held by a boy in cutoff bib overalls next to a large tent looked hard ridden. Pagan must be in conference with Starking. It was time to move.

Walking his horse into the clearing, the AK across his thighs, Trent rode straight and relaxed in the saddle. His hat pulled down to his eyes, the tin star glittered in the sunlight. He noted that this raider camp seemed different from others he had seen. The people at the campfires were bedraggled, and most looked like they'd missed a few meals, but they were clean. The area around the fires was clean, and he noticed for the first time a garbage pit dug to one side, and farther out, the latrine. Someone kept a tight rein on these people. A germ of an idea began creeping into Trent's head.

A wave of people preceded his way through the camp, then broke and split at the large tent as he reined in the gelding.

The curtain brushed aside, and a tall white-haired man stepped outside. Several men, including Pagan Reeves, Ben Hobbs, and Red Seaver, instantly flanked him.

He and Starking took stock of each other, matching what they had heard against what they saw.

The cold eyes gave way to a colder voice. "Speak your peace."

So much for cordial introductions. He looked around the circle of faces, feeling like a bone in a wolf den. If he didn't make this good, he'd have about as much chance.

"Mr. Starking, my name is John Trent. I'm sure the riff raff behind you has told you of me. Assuming that is true, you should know I wouldn't ride in here without good reason. We need to talk. I think we can avoid a lot of needless bloodshed and come to terms that would help us both. If you're willing to listen."

Starking still hadn't looked anywhere but at Trent's eyes. "And why should I?"

He lifted his rifle, causing a hasty stir behind Starking, and then shoved it into the boot on the saddle. Pushing his hat onto the back of his head, he hooked one knee around the saddle horn and gestured to the people around him. "The word is, you want to take Big Springs and make homes for these people. I can sympathize with that. Your people trust you, and I can see you care for their welfare. The problem is, Big Springs is already settled."

Starking nodded. "A few hill people are there, I understand."

Sudden comprehension made him nod. It made sense. "Have you seen it, Mr. Starking?"

The man folded his arms and widened his stance. "Reeves told me about it."

He pinned the man standing behind Starking with a penetrating gaze. "Then you've been lied to." The crowd stirred at this, muttering and shifting their feet in the grass.

Reeves started to speak, but Starking raised his hand to silence him. "Your story is different?"

He turned a little so he could see more people, especially the men and women with small children. "Big Springs has as many people as you do, maybe more. There are families there, just like here. They have a church and a preacher. They have a store that deals in trading, and two grist mills for grinding grain and sawing lumber. There's a ranch nearby that's busy rounding up cattle, and there are enough of those to keep a good many people fat for years. Most important of all, the water at the Springs is clear and clean. The people of Big Springs will fight to keep what they have."

Starking turned back from staring at Reeves. He didn't look happy. "What's your part in this?"

"The Army sent me here to keep the peace, any way I can. I'm supposed to keep the lid on until they can come to the area in force. And they will come. You know what will happen then. The Army's rule is that raiders are shot on sight. I have a better idea."

Starking and his lieutenants bristled at the last statement, some of his men laying hands on their guns.

Reeves pulled his weapon and said, "If you—"

A voice from the crowd interrupted. "Let's hear him out."

Starking called for quiet and got it quickly. "Go ahead, Trent."

"If you try to take Big Springs by force, you'll lose good men trying to take the place, and so will they. It's a natural fortress, and there aren't many ways to get at it. Thing is, you don't need to fight for it. I don't see you folks as raiders, although I can see signs you're headed that way. You just need a place to live. There's plenty of room at the Springs and the surrounding area. If you come peaceful, that is. I'll talk to people and let them know about you. The most important thing is to keep the peace. If people start showing up dead, the deal will be off."

"We get along all right by ourselves."

"Really?" He looked around the circle of faces. "Where are your hunters, Mr. Starking? The forest is full of deer and boar, and the flatlands have cattle running free. I don't see much but rabbits and squirrels in your cooking pots. I see running sores on your children, and they wear rags for clothes. Personally, I don't think you are doing so well. Know why? Someone has all your best men trying to push honest people off their land when they should be putting meat in the pot." The last comment he directed at Reeves, who didn't speak, just raked his hot gaze over Trent.

Starking nodded his head. "I'm told the country around us is hunted out and that we need to move soon."

He shrugged. "Another lie. I had several chances at deer, just riding down the trail to get here."

Reeves, sensing that Starking was starting to listen to Trent, went stomping to his horse. "I'm taking my men with me, Starking, and we'll take care of Big Springs. I can see you don't need us anymore."

Starking's voice thundered at them. "Your men? Maybe we'd be better off without you or your men. Hear this. Whoever quits me and goes with you had better not cross paths with me again. I won't tolerate that kind of loyalty."

Most of the men stayed, while Reeves and a few of his followers left.

Starking turned back to him. "Light and set, Marshal. It seems we have a lot to discuss. By the way, we have one of your Green Jeans in here. He's in a bad way."

Walking into the tent, the smell of rotting flesh assailed his nose.

"Not much we could do for him. He's gut shot." Starking shrugged and stepped away.

Thinking of Gunny, he pulled the blanket away from the man's face. It was Lieutenant Spencer.

"We found him yesterday." Starking was talking again. "I don't know what's keeping him alive."

Lieutenant Spencer's eyes fluttered open. Seeing Trent, he tried to speak.

"What happened?" He leaned close to the man's face, trying to ignore the stench. "Ambush?"

The man nodded assent, finally giving up trying to speak. His breathing was ragged and shallow, fevered eyes holding Trent's.

He thought for a moment. There weren't a whole lot of different ways this could happen. "Raiders?"

At this, Spencer became agitated and feebly shook his head. The effort was too much, and it left him staring with sightless eyes at the side of the tent.

"Guess we'll never know." Starking's voice was non-committal.

He looked levelly at the man. "I'd be real disappointed to find out you had anything to do with this, Starking."

Another voice cut into the semi-darkness of the tent. "Don't get your feathers ruffled, Marshal."

He turned to the entrance, recognizing the voice. It was Gran, the old matriarch from the village he had gone through.

"Do you know this woman?" Starking voiced his surprise.

"I know her." He was smiling. "She kept me from getting shot a while back."

Starking spoke to the woman. "Well, I'm not sure you did the right thing. Today seems to be the day for stories. Let's hear yours."

Gran ignored the man, giving her attention to Trent. "We been scoutin' the hills, like you said to do. Keepin' watch. We run onto that Army patrol you was with, 'cept they was headed the other direction this time. They'd been ambushed all right, but from the inside." She paused to let this sink in. "Someone right in among them cut loose and shot them all. We buried all of them, except for this one."

He tried to absorb his information. There were some in that patrol he wouldn't trust, but would they be capable of doing something like that? He was missing something. *What about Gunny?*

Gran continued in her dry, low voice. "When we found that girl you looked at, Lon saw just a piece of a track. It came from a shoe with an odd stitch. Whoever did the shootin' of the patrol, had that same track. We thought you'd want to know. Don't know if it helps much."

He was lost in thought for a moment. "Did you bury a man with stripes on his sleeves, a sergeant?"

She shrugged, but he could tell he had her attention. "I don't know what a sergeant's stripes look like, Marshal."

"His would have had three stripes pointed down, with two over the top." He drew the figure for her in the air.

"Nope. They all had just one of those stripes."

Relief washed over him. "Then it looks like one got away. Thanks, Gran."

She wasn't through talking. "Marshal?" Trent raised his eyebrows.

"You watch your back, son. There's something not right about this, but we just can't seem to pin it down."

He couldn't disagree with her on that one. "Yeah, I hear you, Gran."

"Then hear this, Marshal. Lon may do the job for you. He was supposed to marry that gal you saw. He's lookin' for the killer awful hard. It's makin' him crazy. Just don't you shoot him by mistake."

"Gran, if you see him...you tell him good luck and be careful."

"I probably won't see him. For some reason, he spends all his time over in this neck of the woods. If I see him, though, I'll tell him."

After she left, he told Starking the story—leaving nothing out.

Starking just shook his head. "Boy, you got a full plate. Talk to your people. Let me know. I've got a lot of people here, and we're all tired. See what you can do for us. Of the ones I can control, I'll keep them in check."

TRENT LEFT THE CAMP, he hesitated to call them raider anymore, with more questions than answers. He had a cold feeling in his stomach that the answer to his questions was staring him in the face, and he just couldn't see it. There weren't many clues, and hardly anything to investigate. So far, all he had were bodies.

Ignoring his wife's death, and thinking only of the more recent killings, there was a thread that was tickling his mind. The only connection between the killings he could see was...himself.

The first girl, found within hours of her death, and second girl, killed in the same manner and near enough to Trent's line of travel to make it an uncomfortable coincidence.

And he was worried about Gunny...where was Gunny? He'd mentioned joining Trent. But maybe he wouldn't. More likely, he was trailing the one who ambushed the patrol.

His mind kept at the problem. So, what did he have?

Two partial footprints of a moccasin that had been torn and repaired, which pointed to a woodsman, and the fact that the man, and it had to be a man, left little or no trail. This fact pointed to someone trained to hide himself. Army? Special Forces? Gran thought the killer had been with the patrol. Had they taken a prisoner? Was one of the patrol members an impostor? And how do you find him in a few million square miles of forest.

Trent's musing had totally occupied his mind, so when his horse pulled up and stopped, he had to look around to get his bearings. The trail, once a fire access road around the mountain, narrowed here with a steep fall on his left side and a high bluff on the right. The path was grown up with grass as high as his horse's knees. Sitting in the partial sunlight that filtered through the trees, he was just nudging his horse forward when he saw a wink of sunlight reflecting off something high on the bluff above him.

He started to wheel his horse when the first bullet caught him high on the shoulder, turning him in the saddle. The second scraped along the top of his head, just under the skin, snapping him off his horse and into the brush along the trail. Head ringing and barely conscious, he kept rolling down the steep embankment trying to get some distance between him and the shooter. Finally, coming up against a lichen-covered deadfall, he lay gasping in pain. The forest fern and grasses were waist-high here, and he couldn't see the trail above from where he lay. Waves of nausea went through him as the initial shock wore off and the pain hit. He shook his head trying to clear his vision, and that just brought on dizziness.

Move. He had to move.

Suddenly the air around him buzzed like mad hornets

as several guns began firing from the trail above. Leaves puffed up around him and clipped twigs and splinters flew into the air, falling on him as he struggled to move. With a huge effort, he rolled up and over the log as he felt two smashing blows in his side and back.

He gave a hoarse cry and went headfirst over the log, fighting for consciousness before he hit the ground. One arm still showed on the trailside of the log, until it slowly slid from sight, leaving a trail of crimson on top of the log.

After the attack, the silence of the forest was nearly total, and the sound of a man laughing came clearly down the slope.

─────

THE STEADY SPATTERING of blood on the leaves was the first thing Trent heard when he came to. His blurred vision could barely see the blood dripping from his nose. He turned and looked painfully at the sun, surprised to see it had moved hardly at all. He must have been out only a few minutes.

Using the log as a crutch, he got his feet under him. Looking longingly up the hill, he realized everything he needed was still up there somewhere with his horse. He had his pistol and the hunting knife. It would have to do.

Trent started to walk...and fell on his face. *All right, I'll crawl. Just like swimming. Reach out and grab a handful of dirt, and pull it toward you...*

─────

THREE MEN RODE out on the trail, having gingerly traversed the bluff. They stopped to survey the damage.

"What do you think, Red?" Pagan Reeves was searching the brush below for any sign of Trent. All they could see was the red-stained log.

"I think we got us one dead marshal."

Shoving his rifle down in the boot, Pagan turned in the saddle. "I didn't hear you shooting, Hobbs."

Hobbs shook his head with a grim expression. "Not much of a back-shooter, Pagan."

"Hell, what's the difference? You're just as dead one way as the other." Pagan eyed Hobbs suspiciously. "You're not gettin' religion on me, are you? I never heard of a born-again raider." Both he and Seaver laughed.

Hobbs pulled his horse back from the trail. "You boys go on to the Springs. I think we'll part company here." His rifle remained pointed at the two men, who were staring angrily at him.

"When you're out, you're out, Hobbs." Pagan's voice was low and threatening.

"Don't try to scare me, Pagan. I don't feel like laughing right now."

After the two men had pounded down the trail, Ben Hobbs sat looking down at the place he knew Trent must be. Sighing, he began a careful descent from the trail into the ravine. Hell of a way to go, he thought, but he could at least bury him. He owed him that much, anyway.

Hobbs approached the blood-stained log. It had taken longer to find it than he first thought it would, and he was anxious to be on his way. Pagan might decide to come back and use him for target practice. Hurriedly he looked over the top of the log. Trent was gone.

With a soft curse, Hobbs quickly looked around for a trail. It was easy to find. Trent hadn't gone far.

The marshal's scalp wound still bled slightly, the rest of his body seemed painted in red. Hobbs felt for a pulse and was shocked to find it—not strong, but steady. He sat back on his heels a moment, thinking it out. He would retrieve Trent's horse and take him to the Sanchez ranch. If he lived that long, so be it. It was too dangerous to take him back to Big Springs. Murdock was not that good of a medic anyway. And Pagan would be there. Nodding his head, Hobbs started moving.

———

HOURS LATER, he was hailed at a sentry post. "It's Ben Hobbs. I got a wounded man here and thought you might want him."

"You are alone, Hobbs?" Cruz had come up silently behind him, holding his short M-4 level with Hobbs's belly.

"I am."

Cruz couldn't hide his dislike for the man in front of him. He knew Hobbs was no good. "And who is this man you think we want?"

"Trent."

With a curse, Cruz grabbed the reins of Trent's horse and began leading him toward the house, shouting rapidly in Spanish as he went. The front door slammed open like a shot and Consuelo came rushing out. Together, she and Cruz pulled Trent from the saddle. His head rolled limply, and his breathing was so shallow they could barely see any movement.

Chico Cruz put his hand gently on Trent's head. "Ah, compadre. It's a poor end. Someone will die for this."

Consuelo was looking strangely at Cruz, never before having seen this kind of gentleness in him. Suddenly, Katie shoved her aside.

"John?" Her hands were covering him, helplessly, touching and probing as tears welled up in her eyes. "God, I've never seen so much blood. How can he still be alive?" Suddenly, Katie gasped, talking to herself. "Oh, thank you, Lord." Now her hands were strong and had purpose. Consuelo and Cruz were looking at her strangely. "Get Murdock. He's going to make it. Look at this." She was sobbing and laughing at the same time. Her strong hands ripped the front of his shirt open to reveal his back and side. "One of the bullets just cut through the meat on his side. It went straight through. The second must have hit a rib as he was turning. The bullet followed the rib around his body and came out the front. If we can keep out the infection, he'll make it."

"He has lost a lot of blood." Cruz was at once skeptical and hopeful.

"I know. But he's strong. He'll make it. He has to." She turned back to Trent. "You crazy, wonderful man. You weren't shot with bullets, you were shot with luck." She was still crying and laughing when she turned to the others. "Come on, let's go. He will be alright. Go."

Cruz sent one of his riders for Murdock with a stern admonition to hurry, then helped carry Trent inside. Disdaining the normal trail, the rider went bursting through the brush heading for the backside of the Springs. He'd probably kill the horse, but this was a friend of Cruz and anyone who crossed Cruz...

Katie was holding him close, covered in his blood, kissing him in relief.

Ben Hobbs clucked at his horse, pointing him toward the gate.

"A moment." Cruz walked out on the porch.

Hobbs reined in.

"Who did this to Trent?" Cruz asked.

"Reeves and Seaver."

Cruz held the man in his gaze. "You were with them."

"I didn't shoot. Chico, I'm not much good, but this I just couldn't do." He paused thoughtfully. "But then, I didn't stop it, either."

"Then why did you bring him back?"

"We had kind of a face-off at the Army base camp a while back. One of my men pulled a gun on him. A dumb kid. Trent killed him. I had my own gun half out of the holster when he turned on me. He could have killed me right then. No one would have said a word. He let me go. I never knew why."

Chico slowly nodded, "It's because he is not the killer most people think." He glanced up. "Are you leaving?"

"Damn right, I am. I don't want to be around when he gets up. That man is gonna be mad."

"I will thank you for him since he cannot do it himself. I'm sure he will not forget your actions. But Hobbs?" Chico's voice turned cold and brittle. "Ride far from this place."

Hobbs walked his horse as far as the edge of the clearing surrounding the ranch house, then went cantering down the trail.

Chico Cruz stood on the porch, foot up on the rail, smoking his little black cigarillo. He knew, with Trent out of the picture for a while, Pagan Reeves might make a move on the ranch. They would have to be very careful. Very careful indeed. He turned to call his men together.

———

IT WAS LATE. The moon had come and gone, and the night breeze coming through the open windows was soft and fragrant. Occasionally, a whippoorwill would call into the night, an echoing answer coming later from another valley.

Murdock had come and gone, and Consuelo had gone to bed. Chico Cruz was somewhere around, but Katie didn't know where. He was always around.

She sat next to Trent, her hands idly playing with his hair, careful not to touch the crease on his scalp. He was lying naked under the blanket—head wrapped in white cloth, along with his shoulder and hip. On his side and in the middle of his back were bruises that were getting blacker by the moment. He had been wounded four times, but with luck, he would make it. *Thank God*, she thought as she bent to kiss his lips.

———

IT WAS DARK AND WARM. There was a fragrance, bringing memories of sweat and passion, something soft and yielding...Trent woke with a start, a jagged edge of pain slicing behind his eyes. "This can't be heaven. It hurts too much." His voice was hoarse and halting.

Katie leaned over and kissed him, not surprised he was awake. She had been noticing signs of him waking up for an hour. "Welcome back." Her eyes suddenly filled with tears again, and she leaned back to keep from dripping on his face.

As he tried to move, she placed a hand on his chest. "Shh. Be still. You'll start the bleeding again."

His memory was coming back in bits and pieces, like looking through a fog. "Where am I?"

She watched him closely. "Connie's ranch. Hobbs brought you here, and Cruz is keeping watch."

"Ben Hobbs?" He gazed at the ceiling, trying to digest that little piece of information. "How bad am I?"

Her hand rested lightly on his arm. "You took a beating, but you'll live. Lost some meat on your shoulder, and you'll have one hell of a headache. You were grazed on the hip, but that's not too bad."

"My chest feels like a horse stepped on it."

"You were hit in the side and back." She moved so she could see his eyes. "I was afraid I was going to lose you. I don't think I could stand that."

He looked at her quizzically. "You're not mad? The last time we talked, I didn't think you thought much of me."

"I gave myself an attitude adjustment."

He sighed and looked at her for a few moments. "Good. I have too much to live for to check out now. I'll be around."

A few minutes later, after she decided he had been kissed and pampered enough, he posed another question. "I can't figure why they didn't come down and finish the job."

"Reeves and Seaver?" Her nose wrinkled in disgust. "Yellow streak, maybe?"

"It'll cost them," he said softly.

"Not for a while, it won't." Her voice was stern. "You

lost a lot of blood, and your shoulder may get infected if you're not careful. It's not too bad right now, but you don't want to break that wound open again. You need your rest."

He digested that thought a moment but realized he was too tired to argue. "What do you hear from Big Springs?"

"I asked Murdock about the town when she came to look at your wounds. She said Pagan rode into the Springs right after he ambushed you. He was really bragging it up." At the look in his eyes, she continued quickly. "Whatever he's doing now can't be helped. The people will deal with it the best they can. It won't do any good for you to go after these men when you're not ready. You would just make it easy for them to finish the job."

He contemplated that for a moment. Through the pain in his head, it seemed like he had to formulate each thought separately and move it silently to the next one. "So, what do we do, nurse?"

"Connie told me of a place not far from here, an old cabin hidden back in the hills. We'll go there and let you mend. They'll let Reeves look around. If you're not here, he won't bother the ranch...we hope. It's the best plan we have."

He tried to sit up but fell back. "And then I'll deal with Reeves."

"No. Then WE will deal with Reeves."

———

THE WATCHER HEARD *the horse running down the trail toward him. He knew it would be the man who had found the marshal. A foolish man to run his horse in the dark.*

The horse screamed as it hit the rope stretched across the trail, stumbling forward and pitching its rider headlong into the dust.

When Hobbs came to, he was standing. How...? He tried to move and found himself lashed to a tree. Looking around, he saw a tall man in buckskins coming toward him.

"Who are you?" Hobb's voice stammered as he tried to control his fear.

"Doesn't matter, boy."

"Wha...what are you doing with that knife?"

"You shot up a good man, boy. You shouldn't have done that."

"I didn't, mister. I never shot him. It was Reeves and Seaver. They did it."

Hobbs was struggling to get loose as the man came closer. "Please, it wasn't me."

"You were there, boy. You were there."

The screams lasted almost an hour. Hobbs was a strong man. A lot stronger than he should have been, or wanted to be. But that's the trouble. Sometimes you just can't die when you want to. The screams were shrill, panting things at the last, feeble and bubbling past bloody lips, but there was no one to hear them. Except for one, and he didn't care.

The Watcher cleaned his knife on Hobbs's shirt. It was hard to find a spot that was not bloody. He caught up Hobbs's horse, took the saddle and bridle off, and slapped it on the rump.

As he watched the riderless horse limping down the trail, he thought of the girl. He could wait now. The killing of Hobbs had sated his thirst for the moment. But he wouldn't wait too long.

———

CHICO CRUZ and one of his sentries stood staring and listening into the night.

"I thought I heard screams, Chico. They were faint, brought with the wind. Terrible screams."

An owl hooted in the distance as the wind rustled the leaves of the towering oaks surrounding the ranch yard. Both men stood for minutes until Cruz finally broke the silence.

"I hear nothing, Jorge."

"But I..."

"I don't doubt you," Cruz reassured the man. "Whatever it was, it's gone."

As they walked back toward the house, Cruz told the man. "Keep a sharp eye. There is a demon feel to this night."

Jorge shuddered as he looked back toward the forest.

FIFTEEN

PAGAN REEVES WAS FURIOUS. It was the day after they'd ambushed Trent, and no one was around. Most of the townspeople had disappeared. Even his men had left the town, and he needed an audience.

Flanked by Red Seaver, he stalked up and down the small street of the settlement, just looking for something to vent his wrath on. He found his catharsis in Reverend Stephens.

Standing in front of his church, the preacher awaited the men approaching.

"Well, if it isn't the Holy Man." Reeves's voice taunted him.

The reverend wasn't impressed. "Leave this place, you're not welcome here."

Seaver had edged around to the side of the reverend. When he looked at Pagan, Seaver drew his pistol and whipped the barrel across the back of his head, turning the blond hair crimson with blood. As the man fell, Seaver and Reeves kicked him repeatedly in the face and ribs.

When they were through, he was barely alive, breathing shallowly through bleeding lips, arms wrapped around his belly, then spitting up blood in a wheezing cough.

Pagan stood over the preacher. "That ought to keep you quiet for a while." He looked at Seaver. "Kickin' preachers is thirsty work. Let's go get some of Murdock's beer."

The saloon had few patrons when the two men entered.

Pagan's eyes fell on Murdock at the end of the bar. "How 'bout bringing a man a drink, Murdock?"

The big woman raised her eyes to meet his. "When I see a man, I'll do that."

Pagan's voice was brittle. "You'll do it now...or I'll burn this place down around your ears."

She handed bottles to each of them. "You know he'll come for you. You gotta know that. This may be the last beer you boys will have."

"Trent?" Red Seaver guffawed loudly. "He never knew it was coming. We hit him twice. He's dead."

"You shot him from ambush? I never figured you for a back-shooter, Red."

Seaver's voice was proud, echoing from the bottle. "It don't matter how we get it done, Murdock. What matters is getting it done. And I never miss."

She gave him a malicious smile. "You did this time."

"What?" Seaver's voice was incredulous.

"I just saw him last night. He'll live a long time. That's more than I can say for you two."

Seaver could not believe it. "We hit him solid. There was blood everywhere."

"Oh, you hit him alright. But you didn't hit him good

enough. If I'm any judge, he'll come to see you boys, and right soon."

"Where?" Pagan's voice was coldly furious. "Where is he, Murdock? We'll just go and finish the job."

"Sure. You go ahead, boys." She rolled her eyes and shook her head. "He's out at the Sanchez ranch. You do know Cruz, don't you? And the rest of his riders? You try anything out there and they'll hunt you down like coyotes."

The two men looked at each other and hurriedly finished their drinks.

They'd just walked out, and Murdock was washing out their bottles when the door opened again. She turned with a scowl on her face, thinking Reeves and Seaver had come back in. A total stranger stood in the room.

"I'm a thirsty man." The newcomer seemed mesmerized as he looked at a six-foot vision of loveliness. "I'm Charlie Walsh, and I ain't had a drink since I left base camp. If you'd trot one out, I'd be pleased to make your acquaintance. Bring one for yourself."

Murdock straightened up a little, smoothing her hair. "It's been a thirsty kind of day." Pouring a straight shot of skull buster, she handed it to him. Walsh knocked back the drink without a shudder under her admiring gaze.

"Have you seen a long, tall galoot around? He's kinda short on brains, but a likable sort, and he'll be wearing a tin star for a target on his chest."

All her sudden friendliness left like a flock of quail. "Why do you want him?"

The man looked at him with a serious expression. "I'm the best friend he has in the world, that's why."

"Well, now." With her faith restored in her first

impression of the man, she walked over to the front door and locked it. "Maybe we should talk."

———

TWO WEEKS later John Trent stood on the front porch of an earth home carved into the mountainside years ago. Katie's 'hideout' had turned into quite a place. The original owner had outfitted the home with the finest survival equipment money could buy. Unfortunately, it looked like they never got to use it. That's the bad part about survival. It's mostly luck, and luck is a fickle mistress.

A walk-in closet had revealed a treasure of weapons. The rifle rack had produced an AK just like his, along with M-16s and a Colt Sportster that looked like an M-16, but chambered for the NATO round.

There were several handguns racked on the wall, mostly semi-automatics, but way in the back was a Smith & Wesson .357, similar in weight to his Ruger. The load was about like his .45 but the ammo was hard to find. Judging from the stash in the closet, ammo would not be a problem for them in the near future. He hefted the pistol and eared back the hammer. No. The frame was too large, and the gun too heavy. He put it back on the shelf. Maybe Chico could use it.

He straightened as he cast a worried look around the clearing. Katie went hunting this morning, and should have been back before now. He'd give her a few more minutes.

Under her watchful care, his wounds were healing fast. Two days ago, when she went hunting, he saddled his horse and tried to get into the saddle. The first step brought sweat to his forehead, but he made it. Soon it would be time to ride. The thought of Pagan Reeves brought anger every time. *Soon...*

Glancing at the trail, he saw Katie striding up the path, carrying a small Whitetail deer across her shoulders. "Another day, another feast?" He noticed a fine sheen of sweat on her brow, and her breath sounded ragged from carrying the heavy deer. "What would you do if you shot a big one?"

She took a deep breath, stretched her shoulders, and smiled at him. "I don't shoot big ones."

He decided to change the subject. There was no use beating a dead horse...or deer. "Any sign?"

At once, she was serious. "None to speak of."

"I went up the bluff today." He gestured at the peak behind the house.

She looked at him critically. He knew she wouldn't see any blood, because he'd changed his shirt...he'd leaked a little.

"And?"

"With those high-powered binoculars we found, you can see this whole country. It looks like Starking is still in his camp. I was worried he would go ahead and take over the town."

"Pagan still has it."

That startled him. "How...?"

He could tell she didn't want to tell, but then she relented. "I scouted up pretty close to town. Found little Tommy fishing the creek. He let me know. Most of the townspeople are hiding in the hills. Pagan and his bunch are just lying around. They seem to be waiting for something." Her eyes searched his worriedly. "If you go, they'll be all over you."

"I know." He suddenly changed the subject. "Found out something about this place today when I was up on the hill."

Her raised eyebrows asked the question.

"Solar power."

She looked blankly at him. He had forgotten how young she was. "Electricity. You know how they generate it at the mill by turning a generator? Years ago, they perfected a way of collecting the sun's energy and turning it into electricity. All I had to do was clean off the collectors and hook up the batteries." He smiled at her. "Although the batteries are in bad shape, I think there's enough power for a small surprise tonight."

She gave him a puzzled look. "Batteries."

"Yes. They're little..."

She dumped the deer at his feet, and he was surprised at the gruffness of her voice. "Surprise me with this. If you can climb that bluff, you can skin a deer. I'll go clean up." She paused, looking back at him. "I wouldn't want to miss anything tonight."

―――――

LATER THEY SAT on the floor of the living room, their backs against the couch. Content, with venison steak nestled in their bellies. The pale glow of an illuminated dial washed over their features. Although they might still work, Trent had elected not to try the main lights in the house. The old car batteries were still weak, and he wanted all their power for his surprise.

Katie was leaning back against him, sitting between his legs, her long hair smelling sweet and clean.

"What's this called again?"

"A CD player. Compact Disc." He wrapped his arms around her, clasping his hands across her middle.

"And it's just music...no words?"

Earlier, he'd tried to explain the concept. "This isn't some folk singer banging on a banjo and singing through his nose."

"Uh, huh. Well, let 'er rip, old-timer." Slowly the music began filling the room. After a quick and delighted look toward the speakers, she settled back to listen. Minutes later, the power stored in the batteries ran out, and she was wiping tears from her cheek. She turned and looked at him, looking deep into his eyes. "It was so sad."

"And also very beautiful. Just like you."

Her voice was soft. "Why? Why did you do that to me?"

He thought a minute, and the more he thought about it, he wasn't sure he'd made a good decision. "I don't really know. Just so you could hear something of what we've lost, I guess. Maybe I needed to share the sadness with someone. Or, since you're so young," he gave her a squeeze. "I thought you needed educated."

She kept silent for a couple of minutes before she spoke. "It's okay then. As long as we share."

They were silent for a long time, each lost in their own thoughts. Finally... "What's the name of the music?"

"Adagio for Strings, by Samuel Barber." He could see her mouthing the words.

"I'll remember that."

Turning her around to face him, he kissed her tenderly. The kiss lasted a long time. When he finally broke away, she remained with her eyes closed, lips partly open. "I want to make love to you."

She chuckled as she bit him lightly on the lips. "Like on the trail?"

"No, not like on the trail. That was more like sponta-neous combustion. We needed each other. This will be different, and it'll take a long time...maybe the whole night."

They joined and when their lips parted again, she breathed softly into him. "Sure you're up to this?"

Her startled laughter, as he lifted her to the couch, turned into a long, soft sigh...

SIXTEEN

THE WATCHER WAS *proud of himself. It was time, and he had found someone worthy. She had come alone from one of the smaller houses surrounding the ranch of Consuelo Sanchez. A basket in hand she was picking black-berries and stopping to pull collard greens from the bog.*

When she was out of sight from the buildings, he came up behind her and hit her at the base of the neck with the edge of his hand. She dropped like a stone, her basket spilling on the path. Picking her up, her long black hair spilled over the Watcher's shoulder. Close up, she was even better than he had hoped. Barely into her teens, she was nubile and firm, and radiated a freshness he could smell and taste. The Watcher would take his time with this one.

———

"JOHN...?"

"I hear them." He reached for his rifle as he went out on the front porch.

Horses. Single file, and coming up the trail. He stood

just outside the door, leaving it open in case he wanted to duck inside in a hurry. Katie was around the corner of the house and behind the breastworks of a woodpile, making an effective crossfire if they needed one.

They didn't. The first rider into the clearing was Chico Cruz. Behind him were ten of his men, all mounted on magnificent horses. Erect and haughty in the saddle, and sporting more guns than an arms dealer, his men looked tough and competent as they gazed curiously around the clearing.

"Light and set." His traditional western greeting carried across the small clearing.

Chico nodded to him, then shot rapid-fire Spanish to his men. They headed toward some shade at the edge of the clearing, two of them breaking off to dismount and walk into the forest. *Sentries. Bad news.*

Katie, her rifle in a sling, joined them as the two men shook hands.

He could see Chico was troubled, yet the man tried to keep up the social amenities.

"This is a good place—"

Trent interrupted, "What's happened, Chico?"

Chico sighed and took off his hat. He looked twice his age for a moment, glancing first at Katie, then back at Trent.

"On our way here, we found Hobbs. He had been dead about a couple of weeks, maybe. Someone cut him up very bad. One of our men heard screams the night after he brought you in. It must have been Hobbs. Someone laid for him. We found a skinned tree. Whoever it was probably stretched a rope across the trail to trip the horse. No other sign, either, not so much as a bent twig. A bad thing, my friend."

"Can't figure it." Looking at Cruz, he knew there was more. Finding Hobbs wouldn't upset him this much.

"Alvarez." Cruz pointed in the general direction of his men. "His daughter is missing. She was picking berries yesterday." He shrugged his shoulders expressively. "We found the basket. That is all."

His stomach clenched and for a second, he felt nauseous. "And no sign?"

"Nothing." He caught Trent and Katie exchanging glances. "This means something to you?"

It was his turn to shrug. "Maybe. If she doesn't turn up."

Cruz looked toward his men. "She is only thirteen. Sweet, like the honey. Everyone loves her; she is like a daughter to us all. If you know something?" His eyes looked expectantly at them, a mixture of hope and dread. "Anything?"

Katie picked up the conversation. "We know of three young women who have been murdered." She gestured toward Trent, "Going back to his wife a couple of years ago."

Chico looked sadly at them. "Then all I can hope is that she is not found. If we never find her, there will always be hope." His voice hardened. "The one who does this?"

He said honestly, "I don't have a clue, Chico, not one. We just have to wait for the killer to make a mistake."

"Raiders? Reeves?" Cruz was searching for any kind of explanation.

"I don't think so. Starking holds the raiders under tight control. Besides, I don't think that is the kind of thing he would go for. Pagan Reeves? My impression is no. I mean, he could be the one, but I don't see him wasting good womenfolk that way. He'd rather keep them around."

"And if you catch this man?" Cruz asked, watching him closely.

He spoke quietly, meeting the other man's gaze. "Then I'll be crossing that line we talked about."

An unspoken message passed between the two men, thoughts of a conversation in another time and place. Katie watched, a puzzled expression on her face.

Reassured, Chico stood and gathered the reins of his horse. "You will go to the Springs soon?"

"Very soon." His eyes were steady on Chico.

Chico's face lit up in a dazzling smile. "This I would like to see."

The group had remounted and was riding somberly away when another rider burst into the clearing. After a short conversation, Cruz turned and rode back to them.

"We have found her." His eyes were hard, and the muscles of his jaw kept clenching. "Please. Will you come?"

"Of course." Trent and Katie replied together.

———

THE CLEARING WAS SMALL, less than twenty feet across, with vegetation choking the perimeter. The mass of cuts and mutilations in the center of the clearing barely resembled a human form.

The group stopped at the edge of the forest. "How did he find her?" Trent asked.

Cruz gave one of his eloquent shrugs. "Blind luck. He was coming to join us and came across this trail. He followed. The trail comes in here and leaves on the other side of the clearing."

He nodded and then dismounted. "Have the men wait. Let's look around."

An hour later, they stood in the shade of a pin oak, watching the men wrap the girl into a blanket and secure her over a saddle.

Katie wasn't quite patting her foot, but he could tell she wasn't pleased with the lack of movement. "Shouldn't we be following that trail?"

His reply was soft, and he was lost in thought for a moment. "The body looks to be a day old."

She quickly caught on. "And the trail?"

"Today," Cruz confirmed. "There is a boot track at the edge of the clearing. The edges are still well-defined. There was a light rain last night that would have softened the imprint."

"Thanks for the lesson," Katie said dryly.

One of the riders was leading the horse back down the trail to the ranch, with two men riding guard. The rest looked expectantly at him.

He sighed, feeling this was the start of an avalanche with no end in sight and no stopping it. "So? Let's go see." He was on point, with Cruz and Katie close behind. The dense growth was too hard to ride through, and the men walked, leading their horses. The trail wasn't hard to follow, a rock turned over here, scuff marks somewhere else. Stopping a moment, he stood listening. The only sounds he could hear were from the men and animals behind him. As always, when trailing, he wished he were alone. "He's pushing too hard."

"I think we have the same thoughts, amigo." Cruz

had come to stand by him. Both gazed down at the barely discernible trail.

"You think someone came up to the body, then heard or saw someone, and went after them."

Cruz nodded with a grim expression. "The trail ahead is made for ambush. We must be very careful."

The trail in front of them blended into a path that wound around the side of a mountain, closed in by dense brush and trees on both sides. The path was barely visible and used only by the animals of the forest. The trees overhead let in filtered sunlight, just enough to make shadows dark enough to hide in. As they rounded a pile of rock, brought up against some trees during a landslide long ago, he saw the body.

"Damn." Holding his hand up, he instructed the party to stay back as he went on alone.

He kneeled beside the man, amazed he was still alive, then propped him up against a tree trunk. When he moved him, he found the courier pouch the man had hidden beneath himself. He slung it around his own shoulder out of habit.

The knife wound in the victim's belly was amazingly bloodless, but already the smell was overwhelming.

Grabbing feebly at his arm, the courier tried to form words his lips couldn't master. Finally, his voice breaking up and faint, he managed to speak. "Trent. I never... never saw him. Had on an Army shirt..."

Lieutenant Saints gathered his strength with a visible effort. Looking at him with feverish eyes, he coughed up blood and his halting voice wheezed as his lungs fought for breath. "It's not supposed to be this way. A man is supposed to die with tall sons by his side and daughters to take care of him."

"You are a good man, Saints. That counts for something." Trent's voice was soft.

The man gave what passed for a laugh. "I've been trying to die...it just won't happen. Can't stand the pain. I'll be crying like a baby in a few hours. We're soldiers, Trent. We've both been in combat. I'm asking for release." The last word pushed past his lips as the soldier grimaced in pain and coughed up more blood.

Chico and Katie had come up behind him.

"You know this one?" Chico asked.

She answered for him. "Isn't he the Colonel's aide from back at base camp?"

He nodded, not moving the hand that was gripping the soldier's shoulder. "Fred Saints. He's Colonel Bonham's adjutant."

"He's still alive." Cruz was looking at the lieutenant.

"I know," he said softly.

"With that wound, it could take days for him to die. But he will surely die, my friend. He would suffer a great deal." Cruz was now looking at him intently.

"I'll take care of it," he said in a soft voice. "It's all I can do for him."

"John," Katie interjected in a startled voice. "There has got to be another way. We can get him back to town. With care...?"

"With care...he would last an extra week." His listless voice was even and unemotional. As a soldier, Saints had made a final request. And whether he liked him or not, he was a comrade in arms.

Cruz put his hand on his arm. "Would you allow me to do this?"

"No. Thanks, Chico...but no."

LATER, as they were standing around at the edge of the clearing, Katie came to Trent. "Why would Saints be here?"

"I don't know, Katherine." His voice was tired. "I do know he and the Colonel were cooking up some plan for moving out here. Maybe he was coming to see me."

He stood with hands on hips as the men with Cruz scouted around the area. They came back with the report he expected. Nothing.

After burying Saints, Katie and the men sat resting beneath the trees. The sun was starting to dip toward the west, and darkness comes early to the forest. It would soon be time to go, but there was a curious reluctance among them to leave this place.

"I don't know. Maybe there is a clue here, and we just can't see it." His voice was skeptical. "I know one thing. Our man is getting a lot messier in his work."

"Which means?" She was still queasy from seeing the young girl, and then Fred Saints.

"Maybe he's losing control. It's possible this has come on him just this past couple of years. If so, he's killing more frequently. It's as if he is feeding on it. But it's starting to take more to satisfy him. He's starting to hurry. And if he is losing control, maybe he'll make a mistake. I just hope I'm close when he does."

She tossed a small stick toward the fire they'd built for coffee. "The words Saints said to you didn't make sense."

"I know. The word: Army. But it made sense to him. I think he was amazed. You know, Saints and I did some training together. He was a good man in the forest, although maybe not one of the best. Whoever killed him laid an ambush and got him cold. Saints never saw who hit him."

A sudden glimmer of light dawned in Trent's eyes. "Maybe that's it. If he wore camouflage, then you might not see him. Maybe that's what he meant by army."

Everyone was looking at him expectantly. "Before the Fall, there was a lot of really neat high-tech stuff in the ranks. I noticed a few of them in the packs of the patrol we came in with."

"Like?" Katie interjected.

"Like a gadget that will tell your position within five feet at any spot in the world, goggles that turn night into day, clothing that changes color like a chameleon. Heat sensors that let you find a man in the dark. You put all that stuff with a man that is an expert in the forest anyway...?"

She was shaking her head. "But there's no Army around here. Gunny is missing, and the Green Jeans patrol was wiped out."

"Maybe. Maybe not." Cruz was unconvinced. "Besides, they don't have to be Army. Anyone could have these things now."

He replied, lost in his own thoughts. "I need to spend some time in the forest. Alone. If I cannot see him, maybe I can feel him, smell him, or even hear him. This has gone on too long. I have to try something."

"What about Reeves? You don't want to have trouble on two fronts. You can't trail this killer if you're worrying about your back trail." Chico's voice hardened. "How about we take care of Reeves for you?"

"No." At the man's startled glance, he held up his hand. "I've something better for you to do, Chico. If your men are willing, pull as many off the ranch as you can spare and put them on the trails. Two-man teams. I want to know who's moving and where they are going. If we see Starking, we'll ask him for help, too."

"You think Starking would help?" Chico's voice was skeptical.

He shrugged and gave a wry smile. "Won't know until we ask."

"And Pagan?"

"No," he said. "Pagan is my responsibility. I'll take care of him. And you're right. It has to be done first." He stood and adjusted his gun belt. "We'll go to town tonight."

———

IT WAS NOT until later that he remembered the dispatch. He opened the courier pouch and retrieved a short, cryptic message.

> Trent. Moving your way with settlers in one month. If Springs is not suitable, suggest an alternate site to Lt. Saints. Charley Walsh closed saloon. Probably coming your way. Resp. Col. Bonham.

So, that was it. More settlers. He sighed tiredly, then in frustration, balled up the paper and sent it winging into the bushes. This wilderness haven was going to be knee-deep in people before long, many of them young women, no doubt. And the killer was still loose with a target-rich environment.

SEVENTEEN

JOHN TRENT PAUSED at the edge of the valley, testing the air like a prowling wolf. Katie kept glancing at him apprehensively. She knew she was in love with him, but at times like this, the knowledge that she didn't really know him that well stood out in her mind. She could feel the rage that was pushing him, and prayed he would survive the coming days.

The night was warm and muggy. Their clothes felt damp in the cloying heat. An occasional flash of lightning would briefly illuminate the sky to the west, and a low growl of thunder would follow.

They walked silently through the glade, moving toward the back of Murdock's saloon. He'd tried to persuade Katie to stay away, but she'd stubbornly insisted. They found the back door locked, but as they turned to go around the building, it opened a crack, creaking slightly in the stillness.

Murdock's husky voice broke the stillness of the night. "Get in here. We've been expecting you." When the door closed again, she turned up an oil lamp and looked them over. "Must have been one hell of a week."

He looked toward the front of the saloon. "I'm looking for Pagan."

Murdock ignored him and smiled. "Trent, you look like you been caught in a stampede of Arkansas Razorbacks, and Katie looks like the cat that ate the canary. I'd say the negotiating is over between you two?"

He ignored her baiting. "Is Pagan here?"

"Nope," the big woman said. "Just some of his boys. Red Seaver is in there, and Jumbo Smith. Jumbo is about the same size as Big Waters, only meaner. You'll notice by the names they use, they ain't the sharpest knives in the drawer."

Trent looked in question at her.

"Big Waters is the one that walks on crutches now, being as someone got mad and broke his leg." Murdock's voice was quiet and sarcastic at the same time.

Katie broke in. "Have you seen my father?"

"I don't know how to make this easy, girl." Murdock reached out and brought Katie to her in a hug. "Hon, your father always was a stubborn man. He met up with Pagan and Red a few days ago. After they beat him around a bit, they came to the saloon. Red went back out and shot him. I am sorry, Katie. He's dead."

Katie went pale in the subdued light. Her eyes went round, then closed in pain. "I should have stayed." Her breath caught in a stifled sob. "I should've been here."

"Wouldna helped none. The preacher's whole flock was around. They didn't help none either. We buried him behind the church, thought that'd be best." Murdock continued to hold Katie as tears coursed down both their cheeks.

"Hey." Murdock grabbed Trent's arm. "By the way, some no-good bum is out there. He claims to know you. Name's Walsh. Pesky little fella. I kinda took a shine to him, so don't shoot him."

He turned his stony gaze toward the door.

"You two stay here." He opened the door a crack and then turned and asked Murdock, "Where do you keep the Ithaca?"

"Under the bar, about middle way. You be careful, Trent. That gun will take saints and sinners alike."

Slipping through the door into the smoke-filled room, He walked casually down to the middle of the bar, reached under, and brought out the shotgun. He thumbed off the safety.

Charley Walsh was sitting at the far end of the bar. When Trent walked in, his eyes lit up. "Well, if it isn't...?" His comment died as he saw Trent take the shotgun. "Oh, shit." Walsh scooted around the end of the bar and pulled his pistol, watching Trent for direction.

The room got quiet in waves, starting close to him and then expanding on into the room as more people looked up and realized who was there.

Red Seaver sat at a table with two other men. When he looked up and saw Trent, he went two shades whiter.

Trent pounded on the countertop with the butt of the shotgun. He had their attention. One of the men at the table stood up, hands out wide. Trent recognized him instantly. Dake Priest was an ex-courier. He'd dropped out of sight the last couple of years and he'd lost track of him.

"I'm not in this, Trent."

Trent shook his head. "Too bad, Dake. I like to get all my chickens together."

"Now, you got no call to act like that. What happened two years ago wasn't my fault."

"Oh, I know. Someone had to supply the raiders with automatic weapons. Right? Tell you what, Dake. You go stand in that corner, and maybe I won't shoot you."

"You want my gun?" Priest asked.

"Keep it. You can use it if you feel lucky." He moved his attention to the rest of the crowd. "Folks, there's going to be some shooting. If you aren't friends of Red here, you'd better get on outside. If you are friends of his, then stay and join the show. It doesn't matter to me, one way or the other."

"Now, Marshal...you hold on a minute." Seaver was sweating. "This ain't going to be fair. I got this girl in one hand and a drink in the other. You got to at least give me a chance."

The area between Trent and the table cleared out, and most of the patrons filed out the door. The table in front had three men, and standing in the corner was a fourth.

"You men were warned. Not only did you stay, you killed a man. And for what, Seaver? What do you get out of killing that preacher? Was that one fair?"

Seaver stammered an answer. "We were drunk, man. Besides, Pagan started that. Not me."

Jumbo Smith had stood it too long. With a truculent voice, he said, "We got you three to one, Mr. Marshal. Maybe if you drop your guns, we'll let you live for a while."

The bargirl started struggling to get away. It was all the distraction the raiders needed. He could see it in Red's eyes. It was going to be now. He made eye contact with the girl and said, "Drop."

The girl fell as if she had practiced the move for years, as Red's gun was coming up. Trent dropped the barrel of the duck billed Ithaca and pulled the trigger, aiming high to avoid the girl. The two men at the table exploded in a red froth as the number four shot blew through them. He whirled to face the man in the corner as a bullet nicked the top of his ear, and he jacked another shell into the pump shotgun. The Ithaca jammed! He sidestepped up the bar as a second shot went through the side of his shirt, palmed his pistol, and fired. Rocked back against the wall by the expanding slug, the man tried to bring his gun in line. He fired again, and the man dropped, his gun falling from lifeless fingers.

"Left, Trent!" Charley's hoarse scream galvanized him back into action. Jumbo Smith, covered in blood, was coming up from behind the overturned table. Trent dropped onto one knee as Smith's first shot went over his head. Carefully, as if on a target range, he fired one shot. Smith stood stiffly for a moment and then collapsed lifelessly behind the table.

The door opened behind him as Walsh got up from the floor. Katie came in, and with one look at the carnage around the table, slowly slid down to the floor. She sat that way, with her arms folded across her knees, forehead on her arms.

Murdock stood protectively over her, but with a sheepish look on her face as she spoke to Trent. "I forgot to tell you. That Ithaca jams a bit. Needs some work."

He just looked at her.

"I said I was sorry." Her customary belligerence was coming back as she went around the bar to help the bargirl to her feet.

He helped Katie get up. "Let's find a place to hole up for the night," he said gently as he folded her into his arms. "And Murdock?" He pointed at Charley. "Take care of my friend here. He looks a little peaked."

EIGHTEEN

MORNING WAS STILL a promise in the eastern sky as they stood by the preacher's grave. The roar of the water rushing from beneath the mountain seemed muted by the fog. The errant breeze, pushing the mist around the small graveyard, was cool and damp.

"We never got along." Katie's voice was subdued, barely audible above the background noise of the Springs. "I'm sorry for that."

"He died doing what he believed in. Even in the face of death. I heard from some folks he did not give in; he was telling them to get out of town when they took him. I would say that is a fair judgment of any man. He died facing his troubles. That's all anyone can ask." Trent's eyes roved around the meadow and toward the town.

She looked up, noticing where his glance went. "Do you have to go?"

"You know I do."

Her head turned away so he wouldn't see the start of more tears. "Isn't there some other way? There has been enough killing."

"If there was another way, I'd do it, Katherine. There's been too much killing, that's a fact. But there will have to be some more before this is over."

"I'm afraid."

"I know, Katherine. So am I. There's a lot at stake, now."

"I should have fallen in love with some hillbilly and raised pigs and chickens." She sighed and leaned her head against his chest. "I don't want to lose you, John. Not now."

He looked steadily into her eyes. "It could happen. You have to know that."

"Why can't we just ride out of here? Why not just grab our stuff and go?"

"What about little Tommy? Or Murdock, do you think she can last—or any of the settlers?" He looked at her, a humorous glint in his eyes. "Don't I remember you telling me I should take this job? It was my duty?"

"I didn't love you then—didn't care if you lived or died. Ah, damn you. I don't know why I stay with you."

He chuckled and pulled her to him. "Sure you do. You said us old guys were more interesting."

She leaned back, looking at him. "You can't do all those interesting things if you're dead."

"Point taken. This won't be a contest, Katherine. Not if it's just Pagan."

"You can't know that."

"I know him. I know me."

———

AS THE SUN started to climb, running the shadows from the street below, people began showing up in small groups, positioning themselves along the street and between buildings for what small protection they would afford. Trust the mountain grapevine. Word gets around.

Leaving Katie sitting on the church steps, Trent was just starting down the hill when he heard his name called. He turned to confront the small group of horsemen just coming in from the trail above the springs. *Just what I need.*

"Mr. Starking."

"Marshal Trent."

He wondered if the thong was off his pistol and vowed to cut it off to reduce that worry. He'd just have to chance his gun falling out of the holster. "I'm asking you to stay out of this, Mr. Starking. It would be a favor."

Starking smiled crookedly. "We never had much in common with Pagan Reeves, Marshal. No, actually, we are here to meet with some of the townsmen. It's peace we're looking for, not war. We won't interfere."

He pulled his pistol, the thong was off, and smiled as several of the men tensed, and then relaxed. He was just checking the loads. "Do me a favor, then?"

If Starking noticed the byplay, he didn't let on. "If I can."

"Pagan still has several men. If I go down, make sure they don't take over the town. There's a future here. If you and your people merge with the settlers, you'll be strong enough that you won't have to worry about the Pagan Reeves of this world."

Starking didn't answer, just clucked to his horse and led his people toward town.

———

TRENT STOOD in the center of the street, with the sun warm on his shoulders. The morning breeze gently ruffled his shirt and carried a hint of lilac and cedar. At times like these, every sense is incredibly alive, and each breath is pure and sweet, as if the body is trying to savor the last feelings it will ever have. He mentally shook himself. *Take care of business.* This was all for show. The townsmen needed to see the outlaws, or badmen, vanquished. The mercs needed to show everyone who was in charge. It may have an Old West look to it—but it was necessary, even back then.

Pagan Reeves stepped smiling out of the saloon where he had been filling up on liquid courage. Two men flanked him. He felt his blood run cold. One of the men was a small-time merc for hire, always wearing an idiot smile. Trent had seen him around but could not remember his name. The other man was Dake Priest. Priest, the ex-courier gone bad, was now a gun for hire. His mouth turned dry with tension and adrenaline as he willed the knot in his belly to go away. *No one said it would be easy.*

"You're running in rough company, Priest. I should've taken you down last night." His voice echoed between the buildings as he purposefully ignored Pagan.

"I like it rough, Trent." Of them all, Priest was the most dangerous. He'd already figured his odds and planned his moves. Standing slightly behind the other two, Priest knew he was in the best position to get a shot off.

"Way I've got it figured, Priest, my first two shots will be for you. At this range, I won't miss. The next shot will be for smiley, there. I'll save Pagan for last."

As he kept staring at Priest and steadily advancing

toward them, the gunman began to get nervous, eyes darting side to side. This wasn't going the way it should. They should stop. Square off. They should taunt each other. This way, and at this range, they would all be killed.

Pagan could not stand it anymore.

"What about me, Trent? Ain't you worried about me? Don't you want me?"

When his left foot hit the ground, he pulled his pistol. "How about now, Pagan?" His gun was up and firing. Priest took one in the shoulder as he dove for cover. The other merc, his hand on his gun, was looking down at the small hole in his chest. Bright red blood was pumping out of his shirt. He started to say something, but ran out of time. He folded up and fell in the dust.

Trent brought his gun to bear on Pagan. Pagan's hand was on his gun, but he hadn't drawn it. It was too late.

"Don't shoot, Trent." Pagan's eyes were ferreting from side to side, desperately looking for help.

Trent just stared at him, while keeping track of Priest at the same time. A sudden shot rang out, and Priest flopped from behind a boardwalk.

The musical voice of Chico Cruz said, "We'll watch your back, compadre. You have a trial to do, yes?"

A trial. Yes.

"How many people have you killed in these hills, Pagan? How much grief and pain have you caused?"

Sweat dripped from Pagan's face, his eyes locked on Trent in a vain hope of reprieve. "I'll leave. You'll never see me again."

"No, Pagan, you'll not be leaving. It's too late. You have Rev. Stephens to answer for and the McCracken family. God knows how many others."

"You're the law, Trent. You have rules. You can't just…"

Pagan Reeves thought he saw a chance. Trent had glanced to the side, and Reeves's hand streaked toward the gun in his holster. Reeves's exultant thoughts were a blur; *I've got him, got him, got him…*

———

THE WATCHER STOOD LOOKING *at the girl in the print dress. Beautiful and willowy, blond hair and large breasts, skin soft and unblemished. Not now. It was too soon. There were too many people. But she was worthy. He could taste her—feel her flesh under his hands. The Watcher drew in a shaky breath. And what of the man? The man he'd come to see fight with Pagan Reeves. He'd known it would be no contest, but three men? And the man was close. He would come for her, come hard! The hero would come for the killer. The Watcher laughed to himself. The hero would not return. So be it. Maybe it was time for that, too.*

Silently, the Watcher moved up behind the girl. She had come in with Starking, but had separated and was walking toward the church and Katie. The girl flinched as shots rang out in the street below, and the Watcher glanced disdainfully in that direction. It would be no contest. The man would win. Would he always win?

The Watcher mentally shrugged his shoulders as he advanced on the girl. It didn't matter. It's the girl that matters. The one who is worthy.

———

CHICO AND TRENT walked back up the hill toward the church, Chico leading his horse by the reins.

"I used to think I was very fast with my guns. Even in this day and age, it is important in some circles." He shook his head ruefully. "Now, I think I'll throw them away. I saw Reeves kill a man on that very street, and I thought he was fast. It's not so. And then, when you looked away from him...on purpose?"

"I had to bait him. Otherwise, he would have crawled away. I just couldn't shoot him in cold blood. Not even him." Trent palmed his gun and held it up. "You know, this isn't something I asked for or ever wanted. I was born with quick hands. Seems to me there should be something better to use them for."

"You did a good thing today, my friend. If you had shown him mercy, he wouldn't have stopped killing. He would *not* have changed."

He thought of all the situations he'd been in, the things he'd done in the name of survival. It was a long list. "In my heart, I know. But in my mind, sometimes I don't know."

A scream snapped their heads up in unison. A girl was struggling with someone in front of the church. As they watched, they saw the man swing, and her head snap back. Katie came rushing around the building, but was knocked sprawling by a sweep of the man's arm. Almost in the same motion, the man swung the girl to his shoulders and disappeared into the forest behind the church.

Cruz was trying to line up a rifle shot when Trent pushed down the barrel. "Too risky."

They both mounted Cruz's horse and arrived at the church in moments, scattering divots of grass and dirt around the porch. A faint trail led away in the wet grass toward the forest beyond.

He wrapped Katie in his arms. "Are you all right?"

"Yeah, I guess so," she answered groggily.

Trent ran to his horse that was tied to the porch. He pulled out his knee-length moccasins, dropped to the ground, shucked his boots, and pulled them on. Pulling his Bowie, he threaded his belt through the loop in the scabbard. Donning a long-tailed hunting shirt, he stuffed trail mix in the pouches. Strapping a Velcro strip over his revolver to keep it tight against his leg, he reached up and took out his AK. Depressing the large silver nub on the top, he folded the stock to make it shorter and then checked the clip. Thirty rounds. It would have to do.

"Let me come with you." Cruz was already turning away to remount.

"No time. I'm going to run him, Cruz. He will have a horse back in the brush. If I push hard enough, he won't have time to stop and hurt the girl. On rough ground, I can make better time on foot. I might even be able to outrun his horse. But above all, I've got to keep him running."

Cruz was nodding his head. "You mean like a wolf pack runs a deer."

He was already looking up the trail, trying to visualize how it would go. "You got it."

"What can I do?"

He held his friend's gaze for a moment. "This may be a long run. If the worst happens and he kills the girl...I'll stay with him. Once I start running him, he'll know that. You and Katherine round up some men and supplies to follow, but not too close. Just stay close enough that I can find you. If I don't get him right away, I'll need supplies.

If you get a chance and can see where he's going, cut in front of him. We don't want to lose him. Not now."

"Then, hurry, man. This man is a devil. You must run like the wind."

He didn't answer...he was already ducking into the gloom of the forest.

NINETEEN

TRENT HIT the edge of the forest at a dead run. For the first few minutes, he would throw aside caution. The girl's life was at stake. He picked up the trail immediately. Broken grass and bent limbs, then the churned grass where the man had mounted a skittish horse. The trail went straight away down a dim path in the forest that would skirt around the mountain. This was second-growth forest, which meant there weren't many large trees, and the grass and bushes were almost waist high.

Keeping his lungs from trying to match pace with his legs, he ignored the burning pain in his chest. He was trying to match the pace of the man ahead. The assailant's first burst of speed would be from the panic of discovery and trying to get away. Soon, reason would set in, and he'd stop. If Trent could keep from overrunning them, that would be his first and best chance.

The initial burst of speed from the man was a lot longer than he expected. It was a full half hour later when the stride of the horse he was trailing began to shorten. Keeping his eyes as far up the trail as possible,

Trent still almost missed the torn grass and dirt clods where the man had reined in his horse and gone off the trail about fifty feet ahead.

The first shot passed with a sonic crack and whapped into a tree behind him. The second creased his hip, leaving a burning red hole in his hunting shirt. Panic shooting? Or a warning? The first came too high, the second too low. He didn't stop, just swerved to the side and into the brush. The growth under the taller trees wasn't thick here, mostly sumac and scattered fern, so he began a weaving approach toward a copse of trees ahead.

Moments later, he rolled into the clearing, bringing his rifle to bear around the perimeter. Nothing. The sun glittered off the bright shell casings ejected into the grass. The man had dismounted to shoot. The imprints in the soft earth were small, maybe a size nine or ten. After the missed shot, he'd mounted and continued down the path, leaving a trail a child could follow. Knowing something of the man he followed, that fact worried him more than anything else did. This man had never left a trail before.

Alright, then. A challenge—and maybe his first mistake.

Standing in the middle of the clearing, breathing heavily, he silently cursed his luck. He hadn't been fast enough. The man was gone...and so was the girl.

He quickly cut three sticks and made a crude arrow in the trail to show which direction he was going. Stepping into the trail, he felt cold fear knot up in his belly. From now on, the man would be more cautious...and he would have to give him the first shot. He wouldn't miss the next time.

An hour later found him on top of a bald knob over-looking the trail ahead. He was scratched and bleeding from the nearly impenetrable shortcut he had taken. His knee-length moccasins had a jagged tear near the top from the fangs of a startled timber rattler that was sunning itself on a limestone ledge. He'd merely ripped it out of the leather and tossed it away. His mind was on the quarry ahead. If the man followed the trail around the mountain, he would have to appear in one of the clearings below. He picked the clearing that had a stream in it. If they would stop for water...

He set the sights of the AK to battle setting for longer range and settled down to wait. Watching the clearing below, he tried to control his breathing. What he was doing was a real gamble. If he guessed wrong and they didn't show up, he'd lose an hour picking up the trail again, and the girl would be dead. If they did show up and he missed his shot, he'd be behind again. It would take valuable minutes to get off the promontory he was sitting on.

———

THE YOUNG GIRL regained consciousness with a rush of pain and nausea. She remembered someone grabbing her from behind when she was at the church. She had tried to struggle and remembered screaming but didn't remember much after that.

Now she was sitting on the ground where the man had unceremoniously dumped her. Her stomach was sore from the ride—from the way he'd draped her over the saddle. She moved to a sitting position and addressed the man. "Mister, don't do this."

"Now you be quiet, missy," the man said. "I don't want to hurt you."

She wanted to spit at him but couldn't find enough moisture in her dry mouth. Her voice came out as a dry rasp. "Like hell, you don't. You're the one who's been killing all the girls."

He pointed his handgun at her. "Hold out your wrists."

When she didn't, he casually reached out and hit her on the side of the head with his pistol.

"Now," he said reasonably.

She held her hands out. Stall. Do what he wants. Anything.

Trent would be coming.

She'd heard her father talk of him. He was like a god to the woods runners. Everyone either admired him or was afraid of him. Stall. He would come.

Seeming to read her thoughts, the man spoke again, laughing. "That boy won't catch up to us."

She turned a defiant face upward. "He'll come, and if not him, my father will. You don't know what you have done, do you? My father is Jeremiah Starking. He can bring a hundred men after you if he wants."

The Watcher, unimpressed by her father's name, turned to face the direction they'd come from. The trail spiraled around the mountain. At points, he could see the back trail. He was about to give it up when he saw Trent drift through a clearing in a long-legged woodsman's lope, head down, rifle in his right hand. Immediately the Watcher snapped his rifle up and fired. And missed.

Trent disappeared into the shadows almost immediately.

The Watcher turned to the girl, chuckling. His body and mouth looked like he was laughing, but his eyes were stone-cold and lifeless. "I believe you may be right. That boy is running, not using a horse. Smart. Knows he can go where we cannot. Yeah, I'd say this is going to be right interesting."

"See? Like I said, mister, you'd better let me go."

Without replying, the man picked her up and put her on the front of the saddle. Mounting behind her, his hands lingered on her thighs and breasts as she tried to twist away from him. "We got to move, missy."

Later in the morning, both the horse and riders were hot and tired, and the Watcher stopped to water his horse. Carrying double in this heat was hard on the animal. Walking upstream from the animal, he braced himself on his hands and leaned forward to drink from the cool water.

The Watcher's reflection in the stream exploded in a froth of mud and water. The man jerked backward as a second round hit the soft earth where he'd been, splattering him with mud. A third notched the heel of his moccasin, taking a bloody piece out of his heel. Whining with fury, he went running and dodging back to the horse, bullets kicking rocks all around him. The girl stayed motionless, hoping to go unnoticed and knowing if she moved, it would hamper the shooter. The Watcher gave her one wild look, stopped, and then threw her on his horse and went pounding down the trail.

Trent stood, cursing his luck and poor marksmanship. There was a sick feeling in his stomach. He had done the one thing he couldn't do. He'd missed.

From behind him came a stampede of sound, and he whirled to see Chico and Katie riding into the clearing at the top of the bald knob.

"You made time, Chico." He was still panting from

the run and ashamed he'd missed the shots. He silently sent a thought of apology to the captured girl.

"I heard shots."

He spoke in a disgusted voice. "I missed him, Chico. I had him, and I missed."

"Shit." Chico's fervent oath said it all. Then he brightened. "The girl is alive?"

He didn't know how long. "So far."

"This is good. Starking is coming behind us, and he's going to kill somebody. If not the man we are after, maybe us. He is mad, my friend."

"I don't blame him." He'd already been moving toward the trail down the mountain as they talked, and Katie was continuing to push him in that direction.

"Go. Go," she cried.

He grabbed Chico by the arm and pointed at the trail. "Where does that trail come out?"

Chico looked down at the trail and then looked around more closely at the mountain. Abruptly, he grinned. "The trail he is on has cliffs on both sides. He has to stay on it until the other side of the mountain. There is a small park that the trail empties into."

Mistake number two.

"How long?" Trent was relieving Cruz of his favorite leather riata as he talked.

Cruz watched him curiously. "Couple of hours."

He put the rope around his chest like a bandolier. "How long to go over the top?"

"For a bird? Not long. But you cannot do it, my friend, even with my fine rope."

"If I can make it over, I can be waiting for him at the clearing on the other side." He abruptly turned to his friend. "Get behind him, Chico. Push him. Not too hard, but stay close enough that he knows you're there. Watch he doesn't double back on you."

He disappeared into the trees before Chico could answer.

———

"CHICO?" Katie's voice was apprehensive. "What if the man we're chasing is Gunny? To me, it's the only thing about this that makes any sense. Gunny is the only person we know who is unaccounted for."

It did make sense. Chico sat looking at her, fear in his eyes for the first time. It might make a difference. Could Trent kill his friend? Or would it slow his hand enough to be the instrument of his death.

Shaking his head and slapping his horse, Chico Cruz went helling down the mountain, making more noise than he'd made in years. Katie was right behind him, pulling the packhorse.

They would push him, all right. Maybe even catch him.

TWENTY

TRENT STOOD at the edge of a clearing, half bent over at the waist, holding his side and taking ragged, deep breaths. His hands were torn and bloody, and there was a long gash down his left side, where he had slipped on a jagged edge of limestone. His hat had gone fluttering down a sheer precipice somewhere behind him.

There was no sign of the man who'd abducted the girl at the Springs. He breathed a silent prayer that he hadn't stopped along the way and prayed that Chico had pushed the man hard enough so that he would be careless.

He didn't have long to wait. With a rustle of leaves and branches, a man rode out of the forest and into the clearing. The man was looking behind him, his face hidden in shadows. It was time.

"Hold it." Trent's voice was level and cold.

"Sure." The man turned in the saddle and faced him. "How you doin', boy?"

"Gunny?" He almost dropped his rifle as he looked back down the trail. "Did you see...?" He suddenly became aware of the girl struggling to get up from where the man had dumped her in the weeds along the edge of the trail.

Gunny sat facing him, hands folded across the pommel of his saddle—and finally, Trent knew the truth. "You."

"I reckon." Gunny just sat, smiling at him.

He was speechless for a moment. In all his wildest dreams, he couldn't figure this. Then... "My god. Why, Gunny?"

"I don't owe you anything, boy. Least of all, explanations."

He almost didn't see the shotgun coming up in Gunny's hands. Throwing himself to the side, he palmed his revolver. The roar of the shotgun was deafening as the shot went high over his shoulder. A couple of the pellets hit him like bee stings. Trent's first shot hit the action of Gunny's shotgun, splintering the stock—the second took Gunny high in the shoulder, punching him out of the saddle.

Gunny sat up groggily in the grass and stuck his finger in the hole in his shoulder. "You like to shoot the lights out of me, boy."

Trent just stood there, his mind still trying to comprehend what his eyes and ears were telling him.

"It's him, John." Katie's soft voice came to him from behind. Chico and Katie had come up during the shooting.

He nodded sadly. "I know."

"Take me to the shade, boy," Gunny said. "I could die in this heat."

He walked up to Gunny and kicked the shotgun away. Reaching down, he relieved the man of his handgun and knife. Pulling him to his feet, he helped Gunny to a pine tree, leaning him against the trunk.

Katie and Chico led the girl away. She was sobbing and cursing in the same breath.

Gunny looked at him with guarded eyes, still trying to bluff it out. "Why'd you shoot me, boy?"

"You had the girl, you were..." he started to say.

Metal and wood clanked at his feet as Katie calmly walked away again. Looking down, he saw a pile of tent pegs and rope. Half hidden in the tangle of rope was a branding iron. A small blackened cross adorned the end of it. His eyes slowly came up to meet Gunny's gaze. "All those women. Why Gunny?"

Gunny slid down the trunk of the tree, oblivious to the blood seeping from his shoulder wound. "What difference does it make, boy? I just do it. Sometimes I remember, sometimes I don't. None of them women was any good. At first, they act as if they don't want it. But they do at the end. They all do. They do anything I want."

"Even my wife?" Trent asked softly.

Gunny glanced away. "Now I didn't know that at the time. I'm sorry about that one."

"You're sorry." His voice became dead and lifeless. "What about Saints and Hobbs?"

Gunny shrugged, then grimaced in pain from the shoulder wound.

The shot startled all of them. Bark exploded from the tree next to Gunny's head, and he threw himself to the side. Coming up off the ground, he saw Cruz taking a rifle away from Starking's daughter. Whipping back around, his hand streaking for his gun, all he saw was empty space. Gunny was gone.

TWENTY-ONE

STANDING IN THE SUNLIT CLEARING, Trent looked past the girls at Cruz. The man shrugged his shoulders eloquently. "I was watching you, not the girl. I didn't think."

Starking's daughter tried to explain. "I'm sorry. I was just mad, I..."

Katie grabbed the girl's shirt front. "Don't you realize what you have done? He's loose again."

"Katherine." His voice was calm as his eyes searched the trees. "It's nobody's fault. We all messed up on this one." He turned to the girl. "Are you alright, Miss Starking?"

The girl nodded curtly. "Yeah, I'm fine. Stupid, but fine."

"Trent." Cruz had been moving around the clearing. "He got his rifle and knife."

He was already thinking of the trail. A man on foot would be a lot harder to trail. "I noticed. He must not have been hurt as much as I thought."

Cruz was having a hard time getting his head around it. "How could he get so much in so little time?"

"We are not talking about an ordinary man, Chico."

Katie had led the Starking girl over to the horses to rest. Walking back, she said, "Something interesting. The girl said just before they got to this clearing, Gunny mentioned they were close to his place. That might be where he went."

He stood looking up the mountain. "Well, now..."

Cruz began walking toward the horses. "We go after him now?"

"Nope." He cast a glance at the sky and the long shadows under the trees. "It's getting too dark. I'm not going into the woods after Gunny in the dark. He would be laying for us for sure." He walked back to the horses. "Better make a fire, and get some food in our bellies. After the meal, put the fire out. We will sleep in a cold camp tonight."

———

LATER, when they were away from Katie, Cruz talked to Trent. "Where do you think he will go? I bet he's long gone from here."

"I don't think he'll go anywhere, Chico. I think he will stay right here and wait to see what we do. He can't chance an open fight, and he won't want to lead us to his camp." His gaze turned to the forest. "I'll go out tonight."

"But you said..."

He shrugged, thinking of the night ahead. "I didn't want to worry Katherine."

"Ah..."

———

THE MOON HAD COME and gone, leaving the campsite a jumble of dark shadows and phantom shapes. The night air assailed the senses, as his eyes tried to penetrate the blackness. Every pore of his body tried to gather information his sight could not provide. There was very little breeze to feel, and the leaves of the trees were hanging limp in the fragrant night air. Trent stood in the darkness, silently adjusting his knife and handgun. He would leave the rifle. This would be close work.

He glanced toward Katie's bedroll, wishing he could run his hand through her hair, or kiss her one more time before he left. But he knew he couldn't. Silence was the key now. It was time to go, and Gunny knew he would be coming. With a slight rustle in the grass, he faded into the forest.

Katie opened her eyes, gazing silently at the place he'd disappeared. Eyes moist and lips trembling, she prayed.

———

DAWN WAS STILL AN HOUR AWAY, and Trent had been completely around the campsite twice. He was beginning to have his first doubts. Maybe he'd guessed wrong. Maybe Gunny was long gone as Cruz thought.

Kneeling by a giant boulder that afforded his back some protection, he stared into the darkness. His senses were like raw nerves, reaching and touching everything, analyzing every sound and smell in the night air. He'd about given up when he felt it.

There was a change in the darkness, subtle and soundless, with a faint odor of sweat and leather. He moved his head, testing the faint breeze, trying to get some kind of direction from a sense only the animals of the forest would understand. The hair on the back of his neck was standing on end, and his breathing was shallow and silent. He was not alone.

It was total darkness all around, and the night felt ominous and foreboding. He carefully shifted his feet, and then froze as he inadvertently made a small crunching sound. A blade swished through the darkness, hanging up on his buckskins before slicing into his leg.

He immediately retaliated, lashing out with his other leg, and feeling the satisfying thump as he connected. The two men came together in the darkness, grunting and straining, both trying for a knee to the groin at the same time, as they groped for the other's knife hand. Over-balanced by the action, they hit the ground rolling, with Trent slashing his knife across Gunny's chest. Suddenly Gunny was up and gone, leaving Trent crouched in the weeds, breathing heavily, nearly deaf to the night sounds from the pounding in his ears. Trent took a long, deep silent breath, forcing his breathing to slow down.

He hadn't heard Gunny coming and didn't hear him leave. Trent shifted his position, pulling a long piece of cloth from his pouch. Knotting it tightly around the cut on his leg, his hand slipped on the bloody cloth and hit a bush next to him.

A stab of flame exploded in the darkness and a three-round burst plowed through the bushes. Gunny had fired at the first sound he heard. Trent rolled from his position and down into a run-off ditch, lined with tree roots and rocks. There was a burning across his left forearm from one of the bullets. As soon as his feet hit the rocks, another burst went over his head into the trees. He palmed his gun, but held his fire, temporarily blind from the muzzle flashes in the darkness.

"Trent?" Gunny's voice carried softly in the night. "You better leave, boy. You'll not catch me out here."

He didn't reply. Taking a ball of string from his pouch, he tied one end to a small rock. Leaning another rock against this one, he started moving softly around to his right, trailing the string behind him. Maybe. Just maybe.

"Not talking, Trent?" Gunny said, chuckling. "Come on. Surely you have questions?"

He pulled the string hard. The tumbling rocks made a sharp click in the night and Gunny instantly fired. Trent palmed his gun and fired into the muzzle flash of Gunny's rifle. The muzzle of the gun flew up in the air, spitting flame into the night sky. Seconds later, he was there, but Gunny was gone. Picking up Gunny's rifle, he melted back into the forest to wait for dawn.

———

KATIE WAS STALKING around the small fire Cruz had started. He'd warned her to stay back from the fire, just in case, but she paid little heed. "We should go out and help, Chico. We have to do something."

"Where would we go?" Chico knew what she was feeling, and felt it himself. But he knew the risks.

In the distance, they suddenly heard the clattering sound of an AK-47, with three spaced shots following close behind.

Cruz stood with his head cocked to the side, listening

intently. "We'll go out when it's light, Katie. Right now, Trent only has to worry about himself. If we went out now, it would be a disadvantage for him."

She relented. "Daybreak then. Is that coffee ever going to be ready?" She looked up, startled as someone was limping into camp. "Cruz...look out!"

———

THE WATCHER STOOD *on high ground, his stocky body easily taking the weight of the tall blond-headed woman. It had been so easy. After all, they were not really woodsmen. They thought he was Trent coming back to the camp. Now he had the girl. Now the man would have to come. The Watcher's interest was piqued when far below, he saw the man come into the camp. It brought back another memory of seeing Trent come into another clearing long ago. Difference was...now he had Trent's woman. Again.*

———

TRENT STOOD at the edge of the small clearing, fighting the impulse to run headlong into the camp. A small amount of smoke was rising from under the steaming coffeepot. His rifle still leaned against his pack and other gear. Lying next to the fire was Chico, appearing at first glance to be asleep--except for the red stain on the earth under his head. Trent still didn't move. Silently he stood in the shadows, eyes probing every possible hiding place around the perimeter of the glade. Finally, he stepped into the clearing, reading the story in the scuffled dirt around the fire. Katie was gone.

"Gunnyyyyyyy..." His voice rocked the mountainside. Anger and frustration tore from his vocal cords in primeval sound, lashing its way up the mountainside toward his foe. "I'm coming for you."

A small sound brought him back from his rage. Chico was struggling to sit up. He turned and kneeled beside him. "Dammit, Chico. What happened?"

Cruz sat looking groggily around. Suddenly his eyes cleared, and he tried to lunge to his feet. "He was here. We thought it was you coming back. He just walked right into camp. Katie yelled a warning at me. That's the last I remember." His eyes searched the camp. "My god...Katie!"

Trent began tying a bandage around the cut on his leg. "He has her. She's gone."

"Then you must hurry. Catch him before he..."

"Not this time." Chico was looking at him as if he was crazy. "He wants to draw me up the mountain. It's between him and me. Katherine is the bait. He won't kill the bait. At least, not now."

Chico started down a trail of self-loathing. "Once again, I have failed you..."

He interrupted him. "Stop it, Chico. We have no time. Do you have men close? Riders you can get to in a hurry?"

"Yes. Yes, I think so." Chico's voice was hopeful.

"Go get them. Seal off this mountain. If the worst happens, Gunny must not escape. No matter what it costs, Chico. Even if Katherine and I both go down, you have to make sure Gunny doesn't leave this mountain." His gray eyes were boring into Chico's. "Is this understood?"

"I will not fail this time." He kept repeating the

phrase to himself as he saddled his horse and went tearing off down the mountain.

Now, Gunny. Trent looked up the mountain. *Now you will pay.*

He faded into the trees at the edge of the clearing, leaving not so much as a ruffled leaf to mark his passing.

———

KATIE CAME AWAKE SLOWLY, reluctant to face the throbbing in her head. Memory came rushing back, and the pain was replaced by fear—a gut-wrenching fear that bolted her upright on the bed, only to be snapped back by the ropes holding her down. She swiveled her head and found Gunny gazing at her from beside a window.

"You." Her voice was full of loathing that somehow did not betray the fear inside her.

"Might as well lay back and be comfortable, missy. It's going to be a long day." Gunny went back to gazing out the window. "That man of yours will be coming up the trail. He will try to get you back. Too bad. It'll get him killed."

Her voice was quiet. "You'll never do it. Not on your best day."

Gunny left the window and came slowly toward her. Katie suddenly realized she was completely naked. Tears formed in her eyes as she fought the restraints holding her to the bed. "Please don't do this, Gunny."

Gunny stood by the bed and calmly cupped one of her breasts. "Do you know how many women have asked me that question and then begged for mercy?" He could feel the heat rising within him. She was so beautiful. Her breasts were large and full and she was so worthy...*not now...not yet.*

She stifled a scream as he pinched her nipple between his fingers. The hand withdrew, only to come back with a glittering blade. Resting the cutting edge on her chest, between her breasts, he lightly pulled the knife down toward her navel—the weight of the knife was the only pressure on her skin. For a moment, nothing happened. Then, a thin line of blood started coming up in little beads of red.

"Oh, he'll come, missy. He'll come and maybe this time he'll kill me. Maybe we'll both go down. But he won't be here for a long while. And missy...by then, you won't care what he does. Not one bit."

———

TRENT STOOD in the gloom of the forest with sweat running in rivers from his body. A thin wire stretched across his leggings—another inch, it would pull free, and the metal fragments from the satchel charge would tear him to pieces. He'd worked his way up the mountain by the roughest route possible. Now, with the cabin in sight, he faced only one way to get to the top of the mountain. It was booby-trapped every step of the way.

Slowly, he backed his leg away from the wire. His heart was hammering in his chest. He hadn't considered booby traps, and he'd almost paid for the omission with his life...and Katie's. *Think, dammit, think.*

He'd just disarmed the explosive charge when the answer came in the form of Cruz. He looked on, astounded as Cruz and two other men were herding a small herd of cattle ahead of them—and coming up the trail. Suddenly an explosion rocked the mountainside, and one of the steers came apart in a shower of blood and hide. The rest bolted, panic-stricken, into the brush. Two more men came up the trail, pushing more cattle ahead of them. Bovine minesweeping was cruel but effective and something used in past war and conflicts. Two more explosions and the men came up even with Trent.

Cruz grinned at Trent. "It's all I could think of, and the trail just looked too inviting."

"Chico, how many more cattle down below?"

"Many more, my friend, and my riders have found a way up the other side of the mountain."

He nodded. "We have to hurry. Gunny will figure out what we're doing. If he thinks he'll have to run, he'll kill her." Trent slid down the boulder he had been perched on. "I need an old-fashioned stampede, Chico. Everything you've got all in one push, right up to the cabin."

GUNNY STOOD BY THE WINDOW, listening intently. He heard three explosions, then silence. "That boy's smart." He turned and walked toward Katie. "He's trying to find all my satchel charges so he can explode them. Smart, but it'll take him too long." He stood by her side, rubbing the side of the blade against her abdomen. "Right now, it's time for us to..." His voice trailed off abruptly.

The sounds of bawling cattle, shots fired, and men yelling signaled the start of the stampede. Chico's men drove the panicked cattle straight up the mountain trail, causing one explosion after another. Gunny leaped to the window in time to see what was left of the herd of cattle already pouring into the clearing around his cabin. Turning, he looked out the back window of the house to see riders coming in through the trees. Cursing, Gunny grabbed his rifle and threw open the front door. Bringing his rifle up to fire, a charging horse knocked him sprawling. He came up firing, emptying saddles all around him. His AK-47 clacked open, and he threw it from him. Pulling his knife, he waited for the one he knew would come.

"It's time, Gunny." Trent was softly treading toward Gunny. "It is time for us."

"Come get it, boy." Gunny's face twisted in a snarl. "I'll give you a belly full."

They came together in a clash of metal as razor-sharp knives made deadly designs in the air. A silent crowd on their horses encircled the fighting men, each mesmerized by the fight before them.

Gunny lunged at Trent, his knife slashing across his arm. Gunny stepped back. "Got you, boy." His laugh died in his throat as he backpedaled away from Trent's attack. When they pulled apart again, Gunny was bleeding from several places on his chest and arms.

He waited quietly for Gunny's next move. When it came, it was so fast he barely avoided it. With his blade pushing Gunny's knife aside, he buried his fist in Gunny's belly. Then, when Gunny folded up, he met his lowering head with a rising knee. Gunny snapped backward and hit the ground shoulders first, and then rolled frantically away—fearing Trent would be on him.

He stood quietly waiting again. No emotion showed on his face as he stared at Gunny.

The soldier stood slightly bent over, his left hand

against his side. "That was good, real good. But not good enough. Now it's time for you to go, boy."

He came at Trent with all his strength and speed until, panting for breath, they stood eye to eye in the middle of the clearing, their knives locked together as they strained against each other. As they stood, Gunny suddenly came up with a knife in his other hand. Trent wrenched away as the blade slid along his side against his ribs, then completed the turn, knocking Gunny sprawling in the dirt. Gunny came up spitting dirt and rushed him. He brushed aside Gunny's thrust and felt his blade bury itself in Gunny's belly.

Gunny looked down at the knife, then up at Trent. His breath was coming in gasps as he looked into his eyes. "Guess I'll go...instead."

"Bye, Gunny." Trent pulled the knife up and over in a figure seven, then pushed the body away. He stood looking at Gunny for a long time, no sound coming from the men gathered in the circle. Finally, the horses parted, and he saw a blanket-wrapped Katie coming toward him. Cruz had cut her loose, and she was running to him, laughing and crying at the same time. As his arms were full of Katie, he looked over her shoulder at a grinning Cruz.

"A long day, my friend." His voice was tired.

Cruz sobered and looked seriously at him. "It will get longer, for us anyway."

Trent, alarmed, pushed Katie away from him. "What is it, Chico?"

Chico gazed down the trail. "We have all this hamburger..."

TWENTY-TWO

THE CRISP, cool air of an early fall day gently rustled the golden leaves in the towering oaks. The day was resplendent in color as the different kinds of trees tried to outdo the other, each trying to be the brightest and biggest.

Colonel Frank Bonham walked past the mass graveyard that chronicled the Fall of the United States far better than the printed word would ever do. He climbed a grassy knoll toward the lone grave at the top. Brushing away leaves stranded against the stone, he placed a small bunch of wildflowers on the grave of his daughter.

Standing again, curious, he reached down and picked up an object lying on top of the stone. Looking around the clearing, wondering who had left it, he finally let his gaze fall on the object. It was a small branding iron with a cross on the end.

He nodded his head once, and then reverently, he placed it back on the stone. Walking back down the hill, his steps slowly regained a youthful spring, his eyes clear and vindicated. His smile—a small thing—growing slowly.

AUTHOR'S NOTE

Big Springs, the principal landmark in this story, is located south of Van Buren, MO, on US 60, then four miles east on SR 103. It is one of the nation's largest springs. Flowing from a collapsed cave, it produces an average of 286 million gallons of water a day.

IF YOU LIKE THIS, YOU MAY ALSO ENJOY: DROWNING ARE THE DEAD

MARK HAYES MYSTERY BOOK ONE BY BRENT TOWNS

BEST-SELLING AUTHOR BRENT TOWNS RETURNS WITH A PRIVATE DETECTIVE MYSTERY—FULL OF SMALL-TOWN SECRECY AND DEADLY INTRIGUE.

In the middle of Australia's Outback lies the small town of Friar's Lake. It's quaint, quiet, and—more importantly—devoid of crime.

So, when a body turns up with the hallmark signs of a manic serial killer from the past, Private Investigator Trent Jacobs is hired by a town local to find out if Ten Cent—the infamous killer—is back.

But as this once-quiet town begins to unravel, tragedy strikes again, and Trent goes missing.

Thankfully, newcomer Mark Hayes is eager to help out. Until— with every shocking secret that's uncovered, he begins to question whether he can find the killer before time runs out.

After all...beneath small-town Friar Lake's dusty exterior, there are hidden truths of which even the locals are unaware.

AVAILABLE NOW

ABOUT THE AUTHOR

Darrel Sparkman is an award-winning author of novels, novellas, and short stories. He's been included in three western anthologies, worked as a feature writer for *Saddlebag Dispatches* and blogged a short time for *Sundown Press*. His ideas come from a diverse past of serving as a combat search and rescue helicopter crewman in Vietnam and volunteer Emergency Medical Technician First Responder. He has worked as a professional photographer, computer repair tech, and was once part-owner of a commercial greenhouse operation and flower shop.

Darrel is enjoying semi-retirement and finally has that job that wakes him up every day—with a smile on his face.